Paul looked at Samantha for another moment, then he said, "All right, Sam. I'll give you a few days to think." Abruptly, he pulled her to him. It was the first time he'd held her in weeks. His large hands caressed her back, warm through her blouse. The he held her close again. In a low voice he said, "But I swear, if that damned actor hurts you, I'll kill him!"

Kate Daniel

ACCIDENTS WILL HAPPEN

FANTAIL

FANTAIL BOOKS

Published by the Penguin Group
Penguin Books Ltd, 27 Wrights Lane, London W8 5TZ, England
Penguin Books USA Inc., 375 Hudson Street, New York, New York 10014, USA
Penguin Books Australia Ltd, Ringwood, Victoria, Australia
Penguin Books Canada Ltd, 10 Alcorn Avenue, Toronto, Ontario, Canada M4V 3B2
Penguin Books (NZ) Ltd, 182–190 Wairau Road, Auckland 10, New Zealand

Penguin Books Ltd, Registered Offices: Harmondsworth, Middlesex, England

First published in the United States of America by HarperCollins 1992
First published in Great Britain by Fantail 1993
10 9 8 7 6 5 4 3 2 1

Copyright © Kate Daniel and Daniel Weiss Associates, Inc., 1992
All rights reserved

The moral right of the author has been asserted

Printed in England by Clays Ltd, St Ives plc
Filmset in Times

Except in the United States of America, this book is sold subject
to the condition that it shall not, by way of trade or otherwise, be lent,
re-sold, hired out, or otherwise circulated without the publisher's
prior consent in any form of binding or cover other than that in
which it is published and without a similar condition including this
condition being imposed on the subsequent purchaser

For Jim Macdonald
and Debra Doyle,
who opened the door

Acknowledgements

I could not have finished this book without the help, advice, and suggestions of the following people. All the mistakes, of course, are my own.

My special thanks to Katherine Lawrence, screenwriter and friend, for general advice and suggestions on movie-making. Additional thanks for information about film production go to Nancy Holder. Steven Brown of Rope of Sand Productions let me watch them filming and answered my many questions.

Virgil and Mary Mercer of the Campstool Ranch provided me with a look at the other side of location filming and general ranching information. And finally, my thanks to Alta Owens of the Hole in the Rock Ranch, an active member of the American Junior Rodeo Association, for information on rodeo and riding.

ONE

The old green Dodge pickup bounced across the cattle guard and headed down the dirt road to the ranch headquarters. The back was filled with more groceries than Samantha Phillips could ever remember having bought. Sam had spent the afternoon in town with Paul Curtis, her boyfriend, carefully working through the long shopping list. Her mom would soon be feeding more people than just neighbors and relatives who'd come to the ranch to help out with the branding.

The late-afternoon sunlight slanting in through the open driver's window felt warm on Samantha's tan arms. Sam had been born in Arizona and had lived there her whole life; she knew the power of the fierce desert sun. It had streaked her light brown hair with fiery blond and red highlights.

She turned in an open gate, under the sign that said Lizardfoot Ranch. Passing the newly installed trailer that was being used as an office, she pulled up to the ranch house and parked by the kitchen door. Paul got out and reached for the first box of groceries while Sam went into the kitchen. "Hey, Mom! Aunt Sylvie!" The kitchen was empty. Shrugging, Sam went back outside, letting the screen door bang closed behind her.

"I guess they're out, Paul," she said. He had one heavy box in each arm. Hastily, Sam stepped back and held the door open for him.

"No big deal," Paul said. "We can handle it." Sam grabbed one of the boxes from Paul and put it on the table as he dropped the other on the floor.

Paul could handle a lot of things, Sam thought, watching him pick up another heavy load. They were both seventeen, with birthdays less than a month apart. She'd known him as long as she could remember. In the last two years, he'd topped the six-foot mark, and his blocky build was an accurate reflection of his strength. Wrestling steers took a lot more muscle than carrying a few sacks of potatoes.

"I sure hope your mom can handle all those meals," Paul said, picking up a fifty-pound sack of potatoes. "Where do you figure she wants this?"

"In here." Sam opened the door to the walk-in pantry. The shelves lining the small room were filled with jars of home-canned beans, tomatoes, and prickly-pear jelly. In the center was a stack of restaurant-sized cans and plastic jugs. Paul and Sam carried the potatoes and the other groceries into the pantry, finishing just as Sam's mother came in.

"Oh, good, you've got it all put away already," she said. "Thanks, Sammie, that helps a lot. I'm beginning to wonder if this was such a good idea after all."

"I have faith in you, Mom. You and Aunt Sylvie can do anything." Sam grinned at her mother.

Mrs. Phillips shook her head doubtfully. "I'm not so sure. Catering for a movie company . . . well, we'll either manage it or we won't. Standing here worrying about it won't do any good."

They'd been talking to the Hollywood people for several months now, but it still didn't quite seem real to Sam. Making a movie at the Lizardfoot Ranch? The lease money the film company had offered was too good for the Phillipses to turn down.

The film was set on a contemporary ranch. Some of the crew had been setting things up on the ranch for more than two weeks. The office trailer had been installed with electrical and phone lines. Mrs. Phillips and her sister-in-law, Sam's aunt Sylvie, had signed a contract to act as caterers. It would mean serving two meals a day for everyone in the film, cast and crew, plus furnishing snacks and some special meals. Sam was eager for the filming to start, since she was curious about the way a movie would handle her everyday life.

Samantha and Paul went outside and headed for the barn and the new rodeo arena that had been built in back of it. "I want to see what they've been building. Think they'll try to keep you away once they start?" Paul asked.

Sam shook her head. "Dad asked them about that when they were working out the agreement. They can't let just anybody wander around, but after all, it's our land. They're going to be doing a lot in the barns, and even a little bit inside the house. The director took one look at the barn and said it was perfect." She grinned, looking up at the large structure. "Since we aren't moving out, they can't keep us from watching them."

Paul laughed. "As long as they don't try to kick Twigs out of her stall, they shouldn't have any trouble. Or are they going to lease her?" Twigs had been Sam's since she'd been a foal.

"No, they're just leasing a few horses," Sam said. As they passed the barn, a teenaged girl nearly ran into them.

"Hello, Sammie," she said. "Seen Dave around?"

Sam shook her head. Nicole Blakely was the only regular cast member already on the ranch. She'd come out a week in advance of the others to practice riding. The film would use a double for most of the fancy riding, but Nicole wanted to do as much of her own work as she could. Sam had gone riding with her a couple of times. Nicole wasn't a bad rider; she just needed more experience.

Sam could tell by the way Nicole was looking Paul over and smiling that the actress wasn't inexperienced in other areas. "Maybe I can find a substitute teacher for my riding lesson then," Nicole said. "Hi, I'm Nicole." She held out her hand to Paul, who took it, looking slightly stunned.

Nicole had curly black hair and an unblemished olive complexion. She was tiny, only an inch or so over five feet, and Paul towered over her. When Sam had met her earlier, Nicole had seemed like any girl from Agua Verde High School. Now that there was a male around, a good-looking one, Sam was strongly reminded that Nicole was a star who was used to getting whatever she wanted. Nicole's sophisticated flirtation had Paul looking at his feet with a nervous smile. Sam had a hunch he was actually enjoying the attention, but she certainly didn't like it. Sam couldn't blame Nicole, though. Although Paul's nose was crooked from the time he'd broken it coming off a bronc, he was still the best-looking guy at Agua Verde High.

Before Sam could say anything, a blond guy hurried around the corner of the barn. His dark eyes focused on Nicole. "There you are," he said. He nodded slightly toward Paul and Sam but didn't bother saying "hello." "You ready to ride?"

"I'll be with you in a minute, Dave. Why don't you bring the horses out?" Nicole gave him an even more blinding version of the smile she'd practiced on Paul, but it didn't seem to faze Dave. He nodded once more and disappeared into the barn.

"Well, I guess I'll see you around," Nicole said. She laughed, a husky laugh Sam hadn't heard her use before. "Unless Sammie gets smart and hides you away until I leave." Nicole smiled once more at Paul, then flashed a quick grin at Sam before turning to go.

After she left, Paul let out a low whistle. "So that's a movie star," he said.

Sam snorted, and Paul grinned at her. She grinned back, then reached up and pulled down sharply on the brim of his hat. "I should have done this earlier," she said.

He pushed his hat back up. "Wouldn't have done much good," he said, looking back toward the barn. "She sure isn't shy, is she? Who's the guy? He didn't seem too friendly."

"His name's Dave Jeffries," Sam said. "I've just met him a couple of times. He's going to do the double work and trick riding for Tim Rafferty. He's helping Nicole with her riding."

"Wonder what else he's been 'helping' her with?" Paul mused as they walked on.

* * *

7

By the time Samantha and Paul returned to the house, Mrs. Phillips was already placing a platter of fried chicken on the large table. Sam hurried in to wash up and set the table. Sam's father was on the radio, chatting with another rancher. The smell of home-cooked food filled the room as Aunt Sylvie came in with a dish piled high with corn on the cob.

The family could still have a quiet dinner now. Soon the Lizardfoot would be buzzing with strangers and Mrs. Phillips and Aunt Sylvie would be too busy catering for the crowd to fix family suppers. As Sam's father put it, right now they were waiting for the storm to break.

"It's going to make things a little rough for a while, keeping the ranch running," he said as the family sat down to dinner. "I'll have to stay out of the way of that circus; they don't want any real ranching showing up in the picture." He winked at Paul and took another ear of corn. "But it'll be an interesting experience, anyway."

"Dad, have you looked at the arena yet?" Sam asked. "I think it'll be great for practicing in." Sam was a barrel racer, but she'd never had a regular arena in which to practice. The movie people had agreed to leave behind the one they built for the film.

Aunt Sylvie spoke up. "Best look around now, Sam. By this time next week, you may not be able to get near it without getting in the way of the cameras. Unless you'd like that." Her aunt grinned. "Ready to be a star, Sammie?"

Paul and Sam volunteered to clean up the kitchen after supper. Afterward, they went out for a walk. They held hands but didn't say much. The pair had known each other all their lives, and had moved into dating without even noticing.

They walked around the end of the airplane hangar, where the ranch's ultralight airplane was kept. The small aircraft were as useful as horses for tracking cattle in rough country. The workmen had just finished putting up a commissary tent next to the hangar that afternoon.

"Looks pretty good," Paul said, tugging briefly on one of the support poles. "What'll they do if we get a bad wind storm?"

Sam sat on one end of a table under the wide expanse of canvas. "Get it down in a hurry, I guess. The movie people paid for it, though, and it comes down when they're done. Not like the arena."

Paul sat down, a casual arm around her, pulling Sam snugly against him. "Now that's something I don't get. Why'd they go to all the trouble of building an arena?"

"I told you—they've got rodeo scenes in the film."

Paul shook his head. "Sure, but—"

She shrugged. "I didn't say it made sense. But they figure if they're going to have rodeo scenes, they have to have an arena."

"Wonder how good Nicole is on the barrels?"

Sam laughed. "C'mon, Paul, you don't think she's really a barrel racer, do you? They've got a double to do all the hard riding for her, just like Dave's going to ride for Tim Rafferty."

"That's a shame. I wouldn't mind seeing some more of her." It was almost pitch-dark under the canvas, but Sam could still see his teeth as he smiled at her. "Don't worry. She's a knockout, but I'd rather look at you."

He kissed her, his mouth warm on hers for a few moments. Then he drew back. "It's pretty late. I promised Dad I'd go check the tanks on the other side of Lizard Peak tomorrow."

He slid off the table and hauled her to her

feet. They walked back toward the house. "I wonder how much Dave'll have to do," Sam said. "Tim Rafferty's supposed to be a good horseman."

"Have you met him yet?" The star of *West Wind* was eighteen, only a year older than Sam.

Sam wasn't much of a television watcher, but she'd seen Tim Rafferty often enough to look forward to meeting him in person. Tim had been a star since he was a little boy, and had grown up in front of the camera. "I can't *wait* to meet him!" Sam squealed, imitating a groupie. "He's *so* good-looking!"

Paul laughed. "Hey, I'm supposed to be your boyfriend, remember?" He hugged her and after a moment kissed her again.

"I remember," she said softly. Then she grinned. "*You* remember it next time you meet Nicole!"

They walked on. Sam thought about her relationship with Paul. They'd known each other for so long that she wondered at times if they were both just taking the path of least resistance. She'd never even dated anyone else. Paul's voice cut across her thoughts as the couple stopped by his pickup.

"Seriously, Sam, you watch your step around

that dude. Someone was telling me last week he's real bad news for women." Paul looked at her, his jaw clenched. "He's going to be staying here on the ranch. So watch it."

"I'm a big girl now," Sam said. She always got a little irritated when that possessive tone crept into his voice. Paul might be her boyfriend, but he didn't have a brand on her. Her cracks about Nicole had just been teasing, but Paul didn't sound as if he were joking now. "Are you jealous or something?"

He scowled briefly. "I didn't say that. I just said Mr. Movie Star has a pretty bad rep."

Sam sat down on the step-bumper of the pickup. "What's he supposed to have done, anyway?"

"I don't know. I only heard he was trouble."

"I can handle myself," Sam said.

In the light shining from the kitchen windows, she could see Paul's rueful grin as he sat down beside her. He touched her cheek lightly with his fingertips. "You usually can. I just hope this movie dude doesn't need any handling. If he does, I may just have to handle him for you."

TWO

By the following week, the headquarters of the Lizardfoot Ranch had taken on the appearance of a small town. Most of the trailers that had been installed were for equipment and the huge generators required by the lights, but a couple were set up as apartments. The show's star, Tim Rafferty, and a few others preferred to stay at the ranch rather than rent lodgings in town. The other cast and crew members were staying at the surrounding ranches, while the single motel and the handful of bed and breakfast lodgings in the small town of Agua Verde were full.

Monday was the first day of the catering contract. Mrs. Phillips and Aunt Sylvie were used to cooking large meals, but preparing food for a hundred people was a different story. Sam and her father pitched in, but even so it was well after four before the cleanup from lunch was completed.

"Well, it will take a little time to get into the swing of it, I suppose," Aunt Sylvie had said. "We didn't do too badly for the first day." They hadn't, but Sam could see just how much work this summer was going to be for everyone. The reality of the stacks of pots and pans that needed to be scrubbed dulled some of the Hollywood glitter.

Not all of it, though. The famous names Nicole chatted about during lunch reminded Sam that these names were attached to real people. Some of them would soon be at the Lizardfoot. Even cleaning the tables and chopping onions for the next day's goulash failed to kill the excitement.

Tuesday went more smoothly. Frustratingly, Sam spent the meal in the kitchen instead of the serving line. Other than Nicole and Dave Jeffries, she still hadn't met any of the actors. As she hauled the full trash bag of dirty paper plates out to the garbage can, she wondered if the entire summer would pass her by, leaving only memories of dirty dishes.

But her mother took pity on her. "We can manage the rest of this," she said. "Why don't you go check the sodas and snacks, Sam; then that'll be it for you today."

"Thanks, Mom." Sam grinned and grabbed a couple of bags of ice from the huge spare freezer they'd installed. The sodas and snacks were kept in a small van, which would be moved to wherever the cast was filming, so perhaps she'd get a chance to watch.

At the van, she added a couple dozen cans of soda to the galvanized washtub and was pouring the ice over them when she felt eyes on her. Turning around, Sam found a familiar face staring at her. A very familiar one. Tim Rafferty.

She'd seen the handsome features—deep blue eyes and tanned face—often in photos and on television, but seeing them in real life was startling.

He said "Hello," and Sam was even more startled. He sounded exactly the way he did on TV. It shouldn't have surprised her, but it did. It was as though a magazine photo had spoken.

He reached past her and pulled out an already-cold soda. "Want one?" he asked, handing it to her. She nodded, and he got another for himself. "By the way, I'm Tim Rafferty."

Sam had finally found her voice. "I think I knew that," she said, grinning. "I'm Sam Phillips."

"Phillips? Your family owns the ranch?" She nodded, and he went on. "Sam must be for Samantha. Pleased to meet you. Very pleased." He popped the tab on the cola and smiled at her, an appreciative smile.

Since he was staring at her, Sam felt free to stare back. He was shorter than she had expected, only a few inches taller than she was. Of course, she had her boots on, and that added a couple of inches, but a quick glance at his feet showed dusty and authentic-looking cowboy boots on his feet. His golden blond hair, casually pushed straight back from his face, and the strong cheekbones and wide-spaced eyes were more vivid in life than they appeared on screen. Sam remembered reading someplace that cameras tended to flatten people. Tim looked great on-camera; the off-camera reality was spectacular.

"Arizona really does have great scenery," he said, still looking at her.

She shook her head slightly, as though refusing the compliment, and asked him, "When did you get here? No one said anything." As soon as she said it, she wondered if the question was nosy, but Tim didn't seem to think so.

"Just a while ago. I haven't reported in yet." He smiled at her, a smile that made her his accomplice in delinquency. "I got into Tucson early this morning, but I took my time getting here. I've never been to Arizona before and I wanted to look around a little. I could have gotten a charter the rest of the way, but I had my Bronco shipped out, so I drove instead." For a confused moment, Sam thought he meant a horse; then, she realized he meant a four-wheel drive.

"The drive just takes a couple of hours," she said.

"I poked around Tucson a little first. And I didn't exactly drive straight here. It gave me a chance to see a little of the country before I started work." He grinned like a schoolboy who'd gotten away with cutting class. "Once we start filming, there won't be much free time. They'd work me to death if I let them."

"Sounds normal," Sam said, starting to relax. She noticed that Tim's smile had faded. "Around here, if you don't watch it you'll wind

17

up working all the time. I'm lucky, though; my folks are pretty laid back about letting me get things done at my own pace, as long as they *get* done."

"Sounds more reasonable than some directors I know." Tim grimaced slightly as he said this. "Some of them seem to think I should be able to work twenty hours a day."

"Do you think you'll have much free time during this movie?"

"I'll make a point of it," Tim said. "Maybe you can show me around some."

"There really isn't much to see around here," she began.

"I bet I can find things," he cut in, smiling.

"Mr. Rafferty!" a harried-looking man suddenly interrupted them. "We've been looking all over for you," he said, taking Tim by the arm and trying to pull him away. "Mr. Ryder's getting angr . . . that is, Mr. Ryder was concerned when you didn't arrive by noon."

Tim shook off the hand that was tugging at him and said, "No one said I had to be here before noon. Go tell Ryder you found the runaway, and I'll be with him in five minutes." As the man started to protest, Tim said, "Five minutes. And please have someone get my stuff out of the Bronco and put it in my trailer."

"All right," the man said reluctantly. "Five minutes." He left as quickly as he had arrived.

Tim turned to Sam, flashing her the quick smile she was used to from TV. "See what I was talking about? It's started already."

"Maybe you'd better go check in," Sam suggested.

"Oh, I will," he said lazily. "But I'll see you later. Remember, you promised to show me the ranch."

"I didn't—" she began.

"Will you?" He reached out and took her hand. "Please?"

Darn him, Sam thought. *He knows just what he's doing. Remember what Paul said about Tim's reputation.* But even as she considered this, she also knew she did want to show him around. He was a flirt and an actor—she'd always assumed that meant a phony. But Tim didn't seem fake at all; actually he seemed like a lot of fun.

"All right," she said. "If you can get the time off."

"Great! And that *was* a promise."

Sam stood there for a few moments, smiling, before she finished checking the snacks.

After Sam had finished her errands for the day, she headed out to take Twigs for a ride. Sam was saddling Twigs when Nicole came into the stable, followed by another girl Sam hadn't seen before. There was something about the new girl that looked weird to Sam. After a moment, Sam realized what it was. The newcomer had green eyes and a very fair complexion, but her cloud of shiny black hair looked artificial and harsh. Artificial was the right word; it was a dye job. The hairdo was identical to Nicole's. Sam figured out who the new girl had to be just as Nicole spoke.

"Sammie, this is Helen Strichek. She's going to be my double. Helen, meet Samantha Phillips. Her folks own the ranch here, so I suppose she's our host." Nicole waved her hand in a vague way, as though completing the introductions. "We were just going out ourselves, Sammie. Helen needs to see how I ride if she's going to look like me. Mind if we tag along?"

In a way, Sam did mind. She wanted to be alone for a while. But it didn't seem polite to refuse, and she'd still get away from the confusion that had engulfed the Lizardfoot. "Sure, come on," she said. "I was just going out for a short ride."

She helped Nicole saddle Pokey, one of the horses that had been leased to the film company. He was a bay gelding, small and compact next to Twigs, a big sorrel. While they got Pokey saddled, Helen got another of the leased horses ready, an Appaloosa. The speed and ease with which she saddled Happy spoke of years of practice.

They mounted and headed north, away from the buildings. Sam had originally planned to head out toward the ridge that marked the boundary between their ranch and the Cradle X, Paul's family's place. It was one of her special places, with an incredible view down Lizard Creek. But with Nicole along, she decided to stick to the easier trails.

Sam led the way up the floor of the main canyon, veering east as they came to a side canyon and riding up along the slopes. They topped a small rise and pulled up. "Wow," Nicole said, pushing her hat back. The wind ruffled her hair and she shook her head slightly to give it greater play. "It's gorgeous up here. Where are we, anyway?"

"We're on the north side of the Little Toe," Sam answered, pointing back down the way they'd come. "The main canyon is called the Lizardfoot, because of the way these side canyons join it. You can't see it from here, but farther down the river if you look up at the mountain it looks just like a lizard lying there in the sun. Well," she added honestly, "it looks like a lizard if you squint a little and use some imagination."

At that, Helen giggled. It was the first sound she had made. Sam went on, "Our brand is supposed to look like the canyon, but I wouldn't try using it for a map."

Helen spoke for the first time. "Sounds like that'd be a good way to get lost."

"Yep." Sam looked at the other girl. "Have you been around ranches much?"

Helen shook her head and said, "No, I grew up in town."

"Give up, Sammie," Nicole advised. "It's like pulling teeth. I met Helen before I came out here, and I don't think I've heard her do five minutes' worth of talking yet. Have I, Helen?"

Helen looked uncomfortable and said, "Well, I don't act. All I have to do is ride, and I can do that."

"Take a look around," Nicole said. "See any cameras up here? Yeah, you'll have to keep your mouth shut when they're rolling, but you can talk now."

Helen smiled again, obviously still very uncomfortable. Sam had never been around anyone so shy. She didn't think Nicole's badgering would help the situation any, though.

"Done much rodeo?" Sam asked. She was thinking of the wall in her room, covered with all the ribbons she'd won competing in gymkhanas and rodeos. Sam knew that Helen had to have a similar background to be able to perform the difficult riding in the movie.

Helen just shrugged slightly and said, "Some." The single word fell flat, and Sam decided to give up on striking up a conversation with Helen. Instead, she asked Nicole, "Have you worked with Tim Rafferty before?"

Nicole's eyes narrowed. "You ever read the gossip magazines?" Sam shook her head. "This is the third movie we've worked on together. We dated for a while while we were making the second one, but I'm steering clear this trip. Professional relations only, thanks. Are you a big fan of his?"

"I don't watch enough TV to call myself a big

fan of anyone," Sam said, "but I've seen him some—who hasn't? I met him just before we came out."

"Oh," Nicole said. She stared at Sam for a moment. There was a little smile on Nicole's face as she assessed Sam. "Oh," she repeated. "Sammie, let me tell you about Tim Rafferty."

"It's getting late," Helen cautioned, and turned her horse around, heading back down the trail. Sam started to follow, but Nicole put out her hand to stop her.

"Tim has a certain . . . reputation," Nicole said. Her eyes were on Sam's, her face intent, but there was something else lurking behind the serious face. Was she jealous? Or just being catty? Sam couldn't figure it out.

"For every new location and every new show, Tim has a new girlfriend," Nicole continued. "I said we dated for a while on our second film. It lasted until we went on location and he picked up some local. He's pretty independent, except for his guardian—you did know his parents were dead, didn't you?" Sam nodded. The plane crash five years before had made headlines. "Anyway, I didn't care much for the way he behaved, and I told him so. We get along fine on-camera, and even off-camera as long as Tim keeps his hands to himself."

"Thanks for the warning, but I probably won't even see him again," Sam said. Even as she said it, she knew she was lying. In her inner ear, there was an echo of Tim's voice saying, *"You promised."*

Nicole brushed the protest aside. "He's seen you; that's enough. You're pretty, and he isn't likely to go for Helen. She's too shy, and she'll be around me too much." Nicole grinned, and this time there was a malicious twinkle in her eyes. "I don't think he'd like that. But it's supposed to be bad luck for the locals he picks up."

Sam pressed her knees into Twigs's side, signaling him to start back down the trail. Over her shoulder, she said to Nicole, "Well, I doubt if I've got much to worry about."

Nicole followed, her low chuckle carrying forward to Sam. "Nothing to worry about at all, if you stay away from Tim."

When they got back to the barn, Helen already had the saddle off Happy. Sam and Nicole unsaddled their own horses and were grooming them when Dave Jeffries came in. Sam could see the similarities between Dave and Tim. They had the same color hair, and were about the same height and build. But Dave didn't have Tim's open, easy charm. Right now he looked irritated, as though some of the burrs they were brushing out of the horses' coats had gotten lodged inside his shirt.

"Helen, Second Unit's supposed to be at the arena in ten minutes. Where have you been?" She started to answer, but he cut her off. "Let's just get over there, before Rick decides to do the stunts without us." He stood there rocking back on his boot heels as Helen finished brushing Happy in a rush. Nicole watched him out of the corner of her dark eyes, but he just continued to rock back and forth on his heels.

When they were gone, Nicole sighed. "Now there's an interesting guy for you, Sam, and just about the hardest one to get to know that I've ever met."

"Have you known him long?"

"I don't know him *yet*, to tell the truth," Nicole said. "I'd like to, but he's about as stiff as my legs feel right now. He's done stunts for a couple of years, but I've never worked with him."

"Take a nice hot bath—your legs will feel better in the morning," Sam advised absently. "Have you worked with Helen before?"

"Nope. I don't know where they got her from," Nicole said. She rubbed at the back of one thigh. "That bath sounds like a good idea, and I doubt I'll get a chance to do much soaking after today. First Unit starts shooting tomorrow. Want to go over and see what we'll be doing?"

On the way to the arena, Nicole explained some of the workings of a production crew. Dave and Helen were both in the stunt team or the Second Unit. The First Unit was the stars, and of course, included Nicole. The other important member of the First Unit was already at the arena, talking with a tired-looking man with a bushy mustache. "That's John Ryder, the director," Nicole explained in a low voice as they approached. "He's a good one, but he's supposed to be so hell-bent on perfection that working with him's a pain. He directed that special with Tim last year."

She broke away and went through the open gate to join the actor and director, leaving Sam standing outside the fence. Sam had no idea what the special with Tim had been. She moved along behind the fence, trying to get closer, when Tim raised his head. He spotted her and smiled briefly, his eyes a warm blue even across forty feet.

". . . a little differently," Ryder was saying. "You'll run across and climb up that fence as quickly as possible, and pause at the top. The camera will be shooting from below, and it'll frame you there against the sky for a moment. It should be a good shot for the title to go on. Then you swing over the fence and drop to the ground. No stunt, just a simple drop of about six feet; we shouldn't need a double."

"I could get along without the double half the time," Tim said. "But I'm not sure about climbing up that fast without losing momentum or looking awkward. Let me try it."

Sam stepped back as Tim and the director continued to discuss the scene, with Ryder pointing in her direction. She must be standing about where the cameras would be for the shot. She grinned. Great! She'd be watching from the right angle.

After another minute or so of talk, Tim broke toward the fence at an easy lope. He moved like Twigs, Sam thought, paying him one of the highest compliments she knew. Graceful and natural. He went up the fence as easily as he had run, making the vertical motion as simple as the horizontal, then paused at the top. Sam was below him, about ten feet back from the fence, and she could imagine what a great camera shot it would be.

Then as Tim shifted his weight to vault over the top the rail snapped under his weight. As the wood splintered beneath him, he had time for one startled yell before he crashed through the remaining bars of the fence. He landed sprawling, his face buried in the wreckage.

For a moment, there was a stunned silence, broken only by the sharp crack of one last rail dropping to the ground. Then people were running from every direction, shouting. Tim sat up, wincing. There was a long jagged cut on his left cheek, where a sharp piece of wood had ripped the skin; it had almost caught the outer corner of his eye. He touched it gingerly, then looked at the blood on his hand in amazement.

As he fell, Sam had started running toward him. She reached him and held out her hand to help him up. He touched his cheek and looked at the blood once more, then took her hand. She pulled him to his feet just as John Ryder and the crew members got there, picking their way past the tangle of broken wood.

Everyone was talking at once, asking questions, demanding explanations and reassurances. Someone handed Tim a wad of tissue to sop up the blood that was dripping off his chin. It was drenched with the dark liquid almost immediately, but he kept it pressed against the wound. Under cover of the noise, Tim told Sam, "Thanks," in a low voice.

There was a peculiar expression on his face, she realized. He was shaken, sure, but there was more to it than that. Anger and surprise and . . .

It had just been a minor accident. But the look on Tim's face was one of pure terror.

THREE

The director tried to keep the talk about Tim's accident to a minimum, but it was still the biggest topic of conversation in the days that followed. Sam had heard some crew members talking about the incident and Tim's injury. They were saying that the actor was a klutz, and that if he didn't watch himself he'd really get hurt. From what Sam had seen, though, it didn't look like Tim had stumbled—it looked like someone had set him up. But soon the buzzing stopped, and life quickly fell into a routine. By the end of the week, it seemed as though the Lizardfoot had been home to a film company for years.

The chow line was the major contact point

between the film people and Sam, yet despite the promise Tim Rafferty had extracted from her, she hadn't seen so much as a glimpse of him since that first day.

The usual ranch chores had to continue just as though there were no movie. Sam spent Friday morning riding along the fence lines, searching for breaks. Her father had spotted several head of stray cattle from the ultralight. He couldn't tell from the air how they'd gotten loose, so a ground-level check was needed. Sam had been happy to volunteer for the chore; not only did it give her a good excuse for a day out on Twigs, but the break was somewhere on Winter Ridge, one of her favorite places on the ranch.

Now, after a steep scramble, she was several thousand feet above the ranch headquarters. The fence running along the crest was the boundary with the Cradle X. Sam let the reins fall loose, allowing Twigs to graze while she looked out over the canyon and the ranch. Here the ridge ran parallel above the Lizardfoot, then dropped in a curve to the southeast and the surrounding foothills. From her vantage point on the shoulder of Lizard Peak, Sam could follow the Agua Verde River almost to its juncture with the San Pedro. The wide horizons of her home always gave her a feeling of solitude and freedom. The monsoons, the annual summer rains, were due in a few weeks. Until they started, the humidity was low enough that sweat evaporated instantly. Arizonans joked about their trademarked dry heat, but the dry air made outdoor work much more bearable when the mercury topped the century mark.

There was a shout behind her. Twigs raised her head and took a few dancing steps to the side as Sam's heels dug into the horse's sides involuntarily. Riding down the fence line toward her was Tim Rafferty. She didn't recognize the horse he was on, a beautiful black gelding.

"I was beginning to think you'd gone some other way," he said as he pulled up beside her. Hastily Sam closed her mouth, aware that it had fallen open. She hadn't been expecting to see anyone up here, much less Tim Rafferty. "Your mother said you'd ridden up this direction and I couldn't miss it, so of course I expected to get lost. I always get lost when someone says I can't miss it." He grinned, the same infectious grin she remembered from a few days earlier.

"There's really not any way to get lost up

here if you stick to the fence," she said, regaining her balance rapidly. She felt less flustered than the last time they'd met. Then she'd been very aware of him as an actor. Now he was on her home ground, under a wide sky; it was easier to see him as just a guy—a very attractive guy.

"Yeah, I can see that," he said, gazing around. His eyes traced the valley almost to the horizon, just as she had done a few minutes before. He took a deep breath, then turned to her with a smile. "This is great up here."

"It sure is," Sam said. She pointed out the landmarks for Tim. Finally, she thought to ask him why he was out riding instead of working.

"I got a few hours off this morning, a surprise. Some spoiled footage from yesterday with Nicole; they decided to reshoot that first. So I thought I'd get you to keep your promise to show me the ranch. I went over to the house and met your mother, but you'd already left."

"Well, this is the best place to show you a lot of the ranch at one time," Sam said. "And not just our ranch, either. Down that way is the Cradle X. . . ." She broke off. Tim didn't notice.

"That's another ranch?" he asked. "I love these names. Who owns that one?"

She hesitated. Finally, after an awkward pause she said, "That's the Curtises' place."

This time he noticed. "Is there something wrong with the Curtises?"

She shook her head, glad she didn't blush. "Paul Curtis is my boyfriend."

"Lucky Paul," Tim said softly. The look on his face made her feel as though an entire swarm of butterflies had invaded her stomach.

"I guess," Sam said. Changing the subject, she asked, "Do they have to cover that up with something?" The gash on Tim's cheek was still visible, even after several days.

He felt his face, gingerly. "Yeah, a good make-up artist can cover scars as easily as make them. It's still sore, but at least it didn't catch my eye."

"I guess next time you'd better take your fences a little slower." Sam meant it as a joke, but Tim didn't catch the humor.

"It wasn't my fault! The thing collapsed as soon as I put weight on it. It was like trying to sit on a breakaway chair—it just fell apart." He touched his cheek again, almost unconsciously. The attractive smile had vanished.

"It probably wasn't built right," Sam said.

Tim's lips tightened. "It should have been," he snapped. "Sets aren't supposed to be that flimsy, especially if you're going to be climbing on them."

Sam realized he was embarrassed. But under Tim's embarrassment, Sam sensed some of the fear he'd shown right after the accident. It made no sense to her, but maybe he was afraid the director would blame him for the fall. "I know it was the fence," Sam said, winning a grateful smile. Tim's weight. "The wood was probably rotten or cracked."

Abruptly, Tim stiffened on his horse. "Look," he whispered, barely making a sound and not moving at all. "What is it?" He was staring past her, out over the canyon.

As carefully as she could, she looked over her shoulder. About forty feet out from the ridge, on a level with them, a large hawk was circling, lazily riding the thermals. Keeping her own voice low, she said, "It's a Harris hawk. Haven't you ever seen a hawk before?"

He shook his head slightly. "Not like *this*. Not this close. It's beautiful." His face was alight as he watched the bird. Then, without warning, the hawk dropped from sight, stooping on some unseen prey far below.

Tim sighed. The small incident melted the last of the tension between them. They started following the fence line again, Sam leading, as they talked of things they'd seen. Tim had traveled, of course, and had seen a lot of what could be called tame wilderness—ski slopes and manicured parks. Still, most of his life had been spent in Beverly Hills and New York. Sam had never been out of Arizona except for a single trip to San Diego, but she had been all over the state and had even been down the Colorado River the previous summer, rafting through the Grand Canyon.

Sam asked him about the big black gelding he was riding. "I don't think I've seen him around before. He's gorgeous."

"He's Worthless." At her involuntary protest, he laughed. "No, really, that's his name. He's mine, and I never get enough time to ride him. Even though we're not using him in the picture, I had him shipped out. I figured he'd like it here."

They were so busy talking Sam almost missed the break in the fence. She pulled up short and dismounted. Heavy branches, probably torn down by the wind, had landed on one of the fence posts and knocked it over. She got her tools out of the saddlebag and started to work.

"You're going to fix it?" Tim also dismounted and examined the fence curiously.

Sam shook her head. "Can't do it right. I haven't got all the tools. It'll need a new post, some new wire." She got the pliers and started freeing the barbed wire from the old post. "All I can do is patch it for now. Here, hold this."

It took about a quarter of an hour for them to get the two strands back up. The trunk of a mesquite tree served as a temporary replacement for the broken post. Tim looked at his watch and swore under his breath.

"What's the matter?" Sam had remounted and was ready to head for home.

"It's noon. Ryder was upset this morning over the foul-up," he said. "I don't need him on my case for being late. I'm supposed to be there in ninety minutes, and I don't think we can make it." He looked back up the trail.

The reminder of Hollywood, of the other activities going on this summer, caught Sam off-balance. She'd almost forgotten about it.

"C'mon," Sam said. "We'll go around." She

nudged Twigs into a faster walk, continuing on in the same direction. Tim, who had turned Worthless and was prepared to head back the other way, called out, "Hey! Where are you going?"

Without stopping, Sam hollered back, "We've dropped so far down the ridge, it'll be faster to cut through the Cradle X and follow the road home." They couldn't push the horses here; the ground was too uneven. But once they hit the road, they'd make much better time.

Within a few minutes the fence made a ninety-degree turn marking the end of the Lizardfoot land. There was a gate at the corner. Sam leaned over and unfastened the wire loop that held it shut, dragged it open, then waved Tim through.

"Basic rule in cattle country," she said, carefully closing the gate behind them. "Always shut the gate." The road ahead of them would tax a four-wheel-drive vehicle, but it was clear dirt and easy riding. The horses broke into a canter, side by side.

The narrow dirt track widened out as they approached the main buildings of the Cradle X. Tim was checking his watch at short intervals now, but Sam was confident there was enough time for him to get back. They were only a few miles from home now.

Sam turned aside onto a well-used track skirting the cluster of buildings that made up the ranch headquarters. They reached the main road just as a battered pickup approached, coming from the direction of the Lizardfoot.

"Sam!" Paul was behind the wheel of the beat-up Ford. He pulled off the road, half-blocking the gate, and got out. Crossing over to Twigs, he stood by the mare's shoulder, gazing up at Sam. Sam could tell he was barely managing to control his temper. Just what she needed. Introducing Paul and Tim would be embarrassing enough, without both of them already upset. Paul's passenger climbed out of the cab, and Sam groaned silently to herself. She didn't always get along with Jackie.

"Tim, this is Paul Curtis and Jackie McBride. Paul and Jackie, Tim Rafferty." As she performed the introductions, Sam wondered what Jackie had been saying to Paul. Jackie was cute, knew it, and enjoyed it too much. She had a way of ruffling Sam's feathers.

"We were just over at the ranch looking for you." He spoke directly to Sam. "Your mom said you were out riding with *him*." The "him" in question raised his eyebrows slightly at the faint emphasis on the word.

"Not really together," Tim said easily. "I didn't catch up with Sam until she stopped up by the fence."

Paul's scowl deepened, and he glared over his shoulder at Jackie. Sam spoke hastily. "I went up looking for the break in the Winter Ridge pasture, Paul. It was under some mesquites; I did a patch, but it'll need to be redone later."

Jackie gave all of them a well-practiced look of wide-eyed innocence. "I must have misunderstood your mom," she told Sam. "I thought you went riding together."

"No, I just followed Sam," Tim said. There was a faint smile on his face as he added, "She's worth following."

Paul's complexion looked as though he'd been out in the sun without his hat. "Yeah," he said, biting the word off. "That's why she's my girlfriend."

Before Sam could say anything about his possessive tone, Jackie spoke. Looking at Tim with an expression Sam was sure she'd practiced in front of a mirror, she said, "I'm surprised there weren't people following you, Tim. It must be great being a star." The smile intensified. "Think there'll be a chance for any of us ordinary people to get a part in the movie?"

That had to be the first time Jackie had ever called herself ordinary. Her father was the county sheriff, an important political job in rural Arizona, and she'd grown up in the local spotlight. She'd earned more attention with her riding. For several years, she and Sam had taken turns at first and second place in barrel racing competitions.

Unlike the guys at school, Tim didn't seem to be susceptible to Jackie's big brown eyes and blond hair. He ignored her melting expression and just smiled pleasantly. "There're a few scenes we'll be filming that may need some extras. I don't know if they're going to hire locals for it or not, though. That's Mr. Ryder's decision." Sam noticed that this time, Tim called the director Mr. Ryder. "You could call the film office and ask."

Tim supplied the number, then looked at his watch again. " 'Fraid that's all I can do," he told Jackie. "Now, if you'll excuse me, I have to get back." He gave Jackie a professional smile and nodded to Paul. "I'll probably see you around."

"Yeah," Paul replied, with a noticeable lack of enthusiasm.

Sam expected Paul to say something to her, but after another wordless look he headed back to the truck. She nudged Twigs into a canter, following Tim. They got back to the ranch with less than fifteen minutes to spare.

As he dismounted back at the barn, Sam heard Tim mutter, "Damn." She knew what he must be thinking. Both horses had big wet patches of sweat on them and needed to be cooled down slowly, then brushed. It would take more time than Tim had. And the horses weren't the only ones sweating.

"Go on," she said. "I'll take care of the horses." She took the reins for both animals.

Tim's face lit up. "Thanks, I owe you one." He sniffed at himself. "I may even have time for a fast shower."

"What happens if you're late?" Sam asked, curious.

"I'm too late right now to answer that." He grinned.

Abruptly, he leaned forward and kissed her, a fast kiss that was over before she was aware he'd moved. "I'll see you later," he promised. Then he was gone, heading for the trailers.

Sam stood there, watching him until he was out of sight. She was tingling all over. She thought about what Nicole had said. *Bad luck for the locals.*

FOUR

Sam got to know more of the film crew over the next few days. Often she'd stop for a few minutes, to watch a scene or chat with a lighting man. One of the actors, Mick O'Connell, reminded Sam a lot of her older brother who was away for the summer. Mick was a good friend of Tim's, having worked with him on several shows. His supply of jokes and puns, all bad, seemed endless. Sam easily fell into a kid sister relationship with him. This was the first summer Jack Junior hadn't been home, and Mick filled the hole left by his absence.

Mick wasn't joking when he came over during supper a week after her encounter with Tim up on Winter Ridge. Sam was refilling the buckets of salad dressing when Mick jogged up. His face grim, he asked her, "Seen the second AD?" At Sam's blank look, he explained, "Gary Hansen, the second assistant director."

She shook her head. "Not since lunch. But Mr. Ryder's over there talking to my aunt Sylvie." She nodded toward a far table where the two sat talking. The director's plate was empty, but he showed no signs of leaving the mess tent.

Mick's face relaxed into a smile. "He seems to be spending a lot of time talking to her these days."

"Yeah." Sam had been surprised by John Ryder's frequent appearances at the ranch house. At first he'd made a pretense of business. It soon became obvious that Aunt Sylvie was the real reason he kept dropping by. "He's over at the house every evening after supper."

"Well, I hate to break things up, but we've had a little accident," Mick said. His smile faded as he spoke.

"What, another one?" A number of things had gone wrong around the set in the last few days. Some of them were minor: an empty film spool, lights dying, sudden noise spoiling a take. But there had been several small accidents as well. A light fixture fell, harming no one but scaring the grip who had been about to move it. A heavy electric cable was left out, tripping the second AD as he hurried around with the daily call sheets. Another cable fell in a shower of sparks during a scene.

"Yeah," he said. "The property master went to check out the loft of the barn and the ladder broke under him. He fell and sprained his back. It's starting to seem like there's a jinx on this picture. I'd better go tell John." Sam frowned to herself. She didn't want to see the movie wrecked by bad luck.

"Hey, it can't be that bad," said a soft voice beside her.

She turned her head sharply. Tim was smiling at her. She'd seen him several times since the ride. Each time there was that warm smile. Sam was uncomfortably aware of how much she counted on it.

"Just talking to Mick about the accidents," she said.

It was Tim's turn to look grim. "Yeah, there've been too many of them. They've all been little ones, but still . . ." He broke off. Once more, she saw a flash of the fear she'd seen in his eyes when the fence broke. Then he shook it off and smiled again. "Think you can get some carrots for Worthless?"

The night after their ride on the ridge, Sam had gone out to the barn on an errand and found Tim feeding a carrot to Worthless. The next evening he had come by the house, asking for an apple. Sam had furnished one, and another for Twigs, and they had gone over together.

Now she nodded. Reaching into the big pocket on her apron, she pulled out a couple of large carrots. "I'll stop by in a while," he said. "Hang on to them till then."

That night they walked over to the barn together. It was becoming a habit. Sam felt a bit guilty when she thought of Paul, but she wasn't really dating Tim or anything. They were just giving the horses treats.

The Fourth of July was coming up, and in Agua Verde that meant rodeo. Sam was the defending champ at barrel racing, but with the excitement of the movie and the additional work of catering and chores, she hadn't spent much time practicing. She got up an hour earlier the next day. If she could do this for the next few days, she should do all right. She'd make up the lost sleep after the rodeo.

Paul stopped by in the afternoon. Sam waited for him to ask her about Tim, but he didn't. It was just as well; at this point she wasn't sure what she'd say.

"Want to watch the fireworks with me?" he asked gruffly. The question was an indirect reference to the fact that things had changed between them; a month before, neither of them would have found a formal invitation necessary.

"Sure. Are you going to be in the parade?" It was a stupid question; Paul always rode with the color guard.

"Yeah." The silence between them was strained, and after a while Paul left. Sam got back to her chores, wondering what she'd do if Tim asked her to the fireworks as well.

When she went into the film office to restock the sodas, Sam immediately saw Jackie McBride perched on the edge of a desk. Mick was explaining something to her as though he was unfolding the mystery of the ages. Jackie lost the rapt student look she had on when Sam came in.

"Sam!" Mick greeted her eagerly. "Come on in. I was just telling Jackie how they figure out which scenes to shoot when." He waved at the strange-looking board behind him. Mick's enthusiasm seemed to be carrying him far beyond the basics.

"The blue dots on those strips mean horses are involved in the shot, so they have to be saddled and ready. The numbers represent the actors; every place there's a four, it means I'm in that scene. And—"

John Ryder hadn't supplied as much detail when he'd explained the concept to Aunt Sylvie and Sam a few days earlier at lunch. "Excuse me, Mick," Sam interrupted. "Jackie, did you ask about that extra work Tim told you about?"

"Mick's positive I'll be in the movie," Jackie said, a touch of smugness in her voice.

"Yeah," he said. "But, Jackie, I told you they'll probably want quite a few people. It's for the rodeo scenes; we need people to play townspeople in the audience."

"Agua Verde's a town. Shouldn't have any trouble finding people to play people." Sam grinned at Mick.

"But some people will just be background, and some people will be real extras," Jackie said. It was clear which group she thought she belonged in.

Mick's appreciative expression made it equally clear he agreed. Jackie had a spectacular figure, and the jeans she had on today looked as if they'd grown on her legs. Even so, Mick warned her, "Jackie, if it was up to me I'd *make* a part for you. But I'm not the director."

Sam had been doing some figuring. "If it's a rodeo scene, we'll need to get Paul and Walt Evans and Mindy Collins. . . . No, her leg's still in that cast."

Mick shook his head. "It's just sitting in the stands. Your friend Mindy's welcome, broken leg and all. It's not going to involve any acting *or* riding."

"Oh." It made sense. "Well, I'll bet lots of people will still want to be in it. Hey, if it's a rodeo, maybe you should come see a real one."

Jackie took Mick's arm as he said, "Jackie's already invited me, and I told the rest of the cast. We'll be there. I promised Jackie I'd cheer for her."

Sam wondered if Mick knew she would be competing against Jackie. Probably not. In any case, he would be there to watch Jackie, not his "little sister." The role Jackie was playing didn't look at all sisterly.

* * *

When the Fourth of July arrived, Tim was glad of the break from filming. The three-day weekend was the first real time off since they'd begun filming. Even so, he had to do a little public relations work. The Agua Verde Chamber of Commerce had asked him to ride with Nicole in the back of a flag-decorated convertible. A news team came out from one of the Tucson TV stations to tape this addition to the Agua Verde parade.

Their car was near the end of the parade, so he got to see most of the rest of the parade. It was a typical small-town parade, the sort he'd thought had long vanished. The Agua Verde High School Marching Band played patriotic songs. Local politicians grinned and waved for all they were worth, including Jackie's father, Sheriff McBride. There were church and scout groups, buggies and wagons dating back to the pioneer days, and floats ranging from simple farm wagons covered with red, white, and blue crepe paper to an elaborate tableau of the Signing of the Declaration of Independence.

Tim waved at Sam as she took her place in the parade line. Sam had braided red ribbons into Twigs's mane and tail, and she wore a blue-and-white rodeo outfit. She waved back at him, then looked around for her old boyfriend. In a way Tim felt sorry for Paul. He seemed like a nice enough guy, but Sam was just too special for Tim to ignore.

This time things were going to be different. He frowned slightly, thinking of the letter. He was still a little uneasy about it. No one had been hurt in any of the accidents that had happened lately, but he wasn't sure how long the luck would hold. And that letter . . .

He pushed it from his mind as the convertible started down the parade route. After the parade was over, he'd look for Sam. Maybe he could talk her into watching the fireworks with him later on. And maybe all the fireworks wouldn't be in the sky. He grinned and waved at the people lining the streets, while his thoughts followed their own path.

After the parade, Sam and Paul went over to River Park, where the smells of the barbecue had half the dogs in town trying to join the party.

Sam sniffed her plateful of barbecue and corn on the cob appreciatively. "Smells good. And I didn't have to help make it."

"Tired of cooking? I thought your mom was

doing most of the food for those movie people."
Paul took a huge bite, then reached for his
drink.

"She and Aunt Sylvie do most of it," Sam
answered. "But I've still done enough cooking
this summer to last me for years. Remind me
not to become a chef."

After they finished eating, they wandered
around the park. It was like every Fourth Sam
could remember in Agua Verde. She always enjoyed the holiday, but this year there was an
undercurrent of tension, and not just from the
competition she'd face later in the rodeo.

Jackie was in the line for barbecue with
Mick. Helen and some of the wranglers who'd
come out from Hollywood with the Second
Unit were playing catch with a softball. Nicole
was sitting on one of the swings over at the
playground, surrounded by what looked like
half the unattached males under thirty in the
park. Sam's nerves flared to life when she and
Paul stopped by the horseshoe pitch and ran
into Tim.

"I wondered where you were," he said.
There was a gaggle of kids trailing him, and
quite a few girls Sam's age were around. Tim
managed to ignore them all without being rude,

the self-defense of someone used to living in public. His special smile for Sam was the same as always.

"Oh, we're just wandering around," Sam said. She tried to keep her voice steady. She didn't want to look like an idiot, even if she felt like one. Paul was her boyfriend—Tim was just a friend, wasn't he? She wasn't used to such high-voltage attention, and she certainly wasn't used to the way Paul was reacting. As soon as Tim had arrived, Paul had turned sullen.

"This is like something from a history book for me. Or from one of those patriotic specials they do for the Fourth." Tim's easy conversational tone included them both, as though he hadn't noticed Paul's reaction. "It's a real community thing here. We have celebrations in Beverly Hills, but they aren't the same." He looked around the small park, crowded with several hundred people from the town and surrounding ranches.

"Well, they couldn't be, could they?" Sam asked practically. "There are almost too many people here, and you've got, what, a million people out there or something? If you think this is cool, wait till this afternoon. More people come out for the rodeo than for the barbecue, and for the fireworks tonight we'll have just about everybody for seventy miles."

"I'll be looking forward to it," Tim said. He smiled at both of them, but somehow he managed to direct it at Sam. Again she felt the flutter of butterflies in her stomach.

"We'd better get going," Paul interrupted. He was scowling. "Have to get ready for the rodeo."

"Sure," Tim said. "I'll see you there." Then he turned and walked away into the crowd.

Sam was a bit embarassed by Tim's open flirtation. As soon as Tim had disappeared, Paul grabbed Sam's arm and pulled her in front of him. "What's up with you and that guy, Sammie?" Paul asked, his grip tightening around her wrist. "I thought I was your boyfriend."

"Paul," Sam snapped. "You're hurting me." She twisted angrily from his grasp and stepped away from him. "There's nothing going on between me and Tim. We're friends."

Paul stared at her. She had never seen him look so angry or cold. "Well, he's no friend of mine," Paul spat out. "Starboy had better watch where he's stepping."

FIVE

Sam didn't notice Tim at the rodeo grounds when she arrived. She did see many of the *West Wind* people—including John Ryder, who was escorting Aunt Sylvie. The announcer made a point of welcoming the *West Wind* crew and asked them to stand up and take a bow. Not everyone was in the grandstand. Earlier Sam had seen Mick by the corrals with Jackie. Nicole was hanging on to Dave's arm. Maybe Nicole was making some progress there. Sam had gotten to know her a bit better. She had learned quickly when it was safe to talk to the pretty brunette. It might be the artistic temperament Sam had read about, but at times Nicole was snappish and bad-tempered, while other times found her full of giggles. Sam liked Nicole, although she didn't really know her, and she wasn't sure she ever would.

Tim arrived just as the barrel racing started. Sam was standing outside the fence with the other competitors, talking to Twigs to steady both the mare's nerves and her own. For a moment she wondered if the timing was intentional; it was practically the first time all day she'd been away from Paul. And with the way Paul was acting, Sam didn't know what he'd do if he saw her with Tim. What Tim had in his hands made her forget the suspicious coincidence. Despite the fact that every store in town was closed for the Fourth, somehow Tim had managed to get a bouquet of daisies. It was a small one, but he presented it to her with a flourish suitable for a dozen long-stemmed roses.

"For luck," he said, smiling.

There was a cheer from the stands as the first rider scored a respectable 18.8 seconds. Sam stammered out a thank-you. She saw Mick and Jackie watching them and felt herself grow hot and embarrassed. Jackie looked as though she hoped there was a bee in the flowers.

"I thought you just gave flowers to the winner," Sam said. She'd never gotten flowers before an event.

"I have." Tim grinned at her.

There was the usual endless wait before the judges signaled they were ready; then, Jackie's horse exploded into motion. This wasn't the beautiful palomino she'd ridden in the parade; it was a paint that ran like it was half-jackrabbit. He was going full speed by the time they passed the electric eye that started the clock.

They got around the first barrel with no problem but swung wide on the second. "That'll cost her," Sam muttered to Tim. The paint's speed between the barrels helped him make up for lost time. Jackie rode him so close to the third barrel Sam was sure he'd knock it over. Then Jackie slapped the paint's rump with the reins as they dashed for the finish. There was a pause, then the judges announced her time: 17.87 seconds.

"That'll take some beating," Sam said, while Jackie exited to cheers and thunderous applause. Jackie was flushed and grinning as she slid off into Mick's arms. There were two more riders before Sam, but there was no doubt whom she had to beat. That was Jackie's best time ever. They watched the next two contestants; then it was Sam's turn. She started to mount and Tim stopped her.

"The flowers were for being the winner," he said. "This is for luck." Ignoring the people all around, he took her in his arms for a kiss. For a moment Sam forgot all about rodeos, barrel racing, and the crowd.

Only for a moment. Then she shoved it deep into her memory. Handing the daisies back to Tim, she swung up into the saddle. Twigs almost danced under her, skittish with excitement. Sam was going to spend a long time thinking about that kiss—right now she had some riding to do. She waited for the signal, not letting herself see the stands, or people, or anything except the brightly colored barrels in front of her.

"Go!" Sam yelped and dug her heels in. Twigs sprang forward, going for the first barrel. Sam pulled Twigs into a tight turn, almost as close to the barrel as its coat of paint. As they came around, Sam's heels dug in again. Sam and Twigs were fast, but on a flat-out straight race Jackie was faster. However, Twigs could almost turn on one hoof, graceful and sure-footed as any dancer. She skimmed lightly around the right-hand barrel and headed for the third and last one. She had the advantage on the turns, if they could just cover the ground between the barrels fast enough to avoid losing the edge.

They were around the last barrel, and Sam lashed across with the reins. The slap signaled Twigs to go for broke. The mare's legs stretched into her fastest run, and the finish flashed by. Sam reined in, easing into a walk and waiting for her score.

Finally the loudspeaker boomed: "Contestant number thirty-eight, Samantha Phillips, with a time of seventeen point five-three seconds. Seventeen point five-three."

The crowd roared, a wave of formless sound that washed over Sam. She choked back a laugh, aware that her cheeks were wet with sweat and tears. She was grinning like a kid. There were three other contestants, but it wasn't likely anyone would beat her time. She dismounted, her legs wobbly, and hugged Twigs just as Tim reached her. Before she realized what was happening, she was hugging Tim and twirling around.

The noise around her dropped suddenly, leaving a pool of quiet in the larger sea of noise. Under her breath, Sam swore, "Oh, *damn*," as

Paul made his way through the group. She didn't want her moment of triumph marred by what she was afraid would come next.

It didn't come. Paul didn't say anything; he just reached out and pulled her into another hug. "Good riding," he said. "I thought you were going to knock that last one over. I saw it wobble."

"Did it?" she asked. Her voice was a little shaky, and her knees felt even shakier. "I didn't see it."

Paul smiled and reached over to pat Twigs's sweaty neck. The smile faded as he looked at Tim. He gave the horse another pat and walked away.

As the next event started, Sam led Twigs back to her dad's horse trailer. When she got there, Paul was leaning against the side of the trailer.

"People have been asking me lately if I still have a girlfriend," he said, fiddling with Twigs's bridle without looking at Sam. "I told them I wasn't sure."

Sam didn't respond immediately. She hadn't had a fight with Paul, and Tim hadn't really said anything. But she did have a clear memory of the way Tim looked at her, and their evening walks to see the horses, and his hand holding hers. And of that kiss before she went into the ring. Paul had always been there, like a part of her; Tim was something new. She didn't know at this point which one she preferred.

"Well, I'm here, aren't I?" Sam offered. It was a cop-out, and they both knew it, but for the moment Paul let it pass.

They went on back to the stands and joined their friends to watch the show until Paul's event, bronc riding. These were the kids Sam had known all her life, her friends, her world. Mindy had her leg in its heavy cast propped across the back of the seat in front of her. Mike Trujillo, a year behind them in school, was cracking everyone up with his running commentary on the events. Walt Evans never shifted his eyes from the arena. Walt was more devoted to rodeo than anyone Sam knew. He planned on turning pro right after high school. There were also new faces this summer. Jackie sat with Mick. Nicole and Dave arrived with Rick Moore and some of the stunt crew. Larry Cabot was talking with Tim, who smiled at Sam.

At first everyone was joking. There were comments about Hollywood cowboys, and cracks about the upcoming rodeo sequences for the movie. Mick urged everyone to sign up as extras. Helen asked Mindy about the fall that had shattered her leg, while Dave explained the differences between movie stunt riding and rodeo work to several of the local guys.

Gradually, an undercurrent crept in that made Sam uneasy. She wasn't sure just how it started, but the cracks about phony danger for phony cowboys began to have a nasty edge. Paul took the lead, needling Tim about needing Dave as his double. Tim, who really was a good rider, got mad.

"I'd ride my own stunts if they'd let me," he snapped after one particularly biting comment. "If they let me, they couldn't get insurance on the picture."

"Insurance?" Paul's tone of voice made the word sound like a condemnation.

Mindy broke in. "Hey, anyone can have an accident," she said. For emphasis, she lifted her plaster-coated leg an inch or two. Since no one questioned Mindy's riding ability, the subject was dropped for a while. Only for a while— soon the nasty undercurrent crept back into the conversation.

Paul's event finally came up. Several of the guys were entered for bronc riding, and they left in a group. Dave had been a rodeo rider himself, and he and the other stunt riders went along to watch from down by the chutes. As they left, Paul told Tim, "You can stay here and watch with the ladies."

Sam boiled. It was straight macho talk, the sort of thing she often heard around the rodeo circuit. As Tim and Mick got up to follow the other guys, she didn't know whom she was angrier at: Paul for playing macho or Tim for reacting to the provocation.

She sat there through the first contestant's try. It was a very short ride; he shot off over the horse's shoulder almost immediately. The announcer's comments about the height he reached before his quick descent were appreciated by the crowd. As the drawling voice continued to boom, killing time before the next contestant, Sam decided to go around to the chutes herself. She stood up and started to inch her way toward the aisle. As she pushed past Jackie, the other girl asked her, "Where're you going, Sammie?"

Abruptly, Sam decided it might be a little easier if there were two of them. "Over to the chutes. Want to come along?"

"Mick headed over that way, didn't he?" Not

waiting for an answer, Jackie stood up. "Sure, I'll come."

"You really getting interested in Mick?" Sam asked as they made their way around the stands.

"Maybe I am. Not that it's any of your business." Jackie was silent for a moment. In a less belligerent tone, she added, "I thought actors would be full of hot air, all phony and stuck on themselves. Mick isn't."

"I know," Sam said. "Neither's Tim."

They reached the chutes just as the starting signal was given and the gate was pulled open. Both girls climbed up on the fence, where most of the guys were perched, and cheered as Paul's horse, a powerful gray stallion, plunged into the arena. The stallion bucked hard but without the vicious sideways twists of some horses, and Paul rode out the time, left hand well away from the leather all the way through. As the buzzer sounded, Paul cleanly made the transfer to the pickup man's horse and came back to the chutes through a storm of applause. His eyes lit up as he saw Sam, and he slid off beside her to collect a fast kiss.

"Paul, that was . . ." She broke off, suddenly feeling chilled. Walt was supposed to ride next.

Instead a grim-faced Tim was on Walt's horse, wrapping the reins around his right hand. "Tim, you can't!" She scrambled up the side of the chute.

"I won't last long, and I know it. Still, it ought to shut a few people up," Tim said. The horse fretted beneath him, its hindquarters shifting uneasily. There was a set look on Tim's face, as though he was going to do this no matter how much it scared him.

It should scare him, she thought furiously. *He has no idea how to ride a bronc. He could get himself killed.*

"Just a short ride, Sam," Tim said stubbornly. "It'll be great publicity."

"I think not." The new voice was crisp and angry. "Having the star break his neck is not the type of publicity I want for any picture of mine. Tim, you ride that horse and you'll spend more time in court than in front of a camera. You signed a contract, remember?" John Ryder stood there, staring icily at his leading man.

Someone tugged Sam's elbow. She turned, then hopped off the bottom bar of the fence. "Aunt Sylvie!"

"What's going on, Sammie?" her aunt asked

67

in a low voice. She looked as angry as John. "What's that jackass think he's doing?"

"Paul rode him harder than he did that bronc," Sam told her.

Aunt Sylvie's green eyes met Sam's. "They playing macho over you, Sammie?" Behind them, Tim was yelling at John, whose voice dropped lower in response.

"It started that way," Sam said. "Like I'm some princess in a fairy tale, with the knights fighting over me. Wonder why the stories never say the princess wanted to kick both of them."

Aunt Sylvie grinned. "Maybe the princess didn't have as much sense as you do. Well, looks as if Tim's got *some* sense, anyway." Tim was out of the saddle and getting onto the side of the chute.

Walt Evans climbed up and swung a leg over the horse, settling into the saddle. Tim, his face flushed, dropped down beside Sam and Aunt Sylvie. The older woman spoke first.

"How'd you get Walt to let you have his ride?"

"I don't remember, someone suggested it and he offered to let me ride his bronc. And I could have, if Ryder wasn't such a damned—"

"Temper, temper," Sylvie said. She sounded

amused. "He was only doing his job, and you know it, Tim. Let's just watch Walt take his ride." Sam was too angry with Tim and Paul to speak to either of them.

The voice on the loudspeaker announced Walt, and he gave the signal. The gate was pulled open, and the horse erupted from the chute.

The instant the horse left the chute, it was obvious Walt was in trouble. The saddle slipped badly as the wild animal plunged away from the gate. Walt, unable to stay aboard, tried to throw himself clear.

There was a sickening crack, audible over the noise of the crowd, as he hit the fence headfirst. The group around the chute ran to Walt's crumpled form. A sudden hush had fallen over the stands. The silence was cut by one sharp scream as John Ryder, his face ashen, straightened up.

"He's dead."

SIX

The accident brought the rodeo to an abrupt end. Friends clung together. Dave, his face pale, had an arm around Helen. Nicole was nowhere in sight. Jackie buried her face in Mick's chest. Sam huddled near them, stunned. After a few minutes, Sheriff McBride hurried up. He gently pulled Jackie to one side and began questioning her in a low voice.

Mick slipped an arm around Sam, as the sheriff moved off with Jackie. For once, Mick's blue eyes weren't laughing. "What the hell happened?" He stared at Walt's limp body.

Sam fought to control her voice. "It was an accident." She paused to wipe the tears off her cheeks. "Walt's too good a rider—"

71

"I don't care how good a rider he was," Mick interrupted grimly. "That saddle shouldn't have slipped like that."

Aunt Sylvie and John were near them. Their heads were on a level, his tilted slightly to listen to her. Sam couldn't hear them, but tears were streaming unheeded down her aunt's cheeks. She'd known Walt since he was a baby, and the accident must have brought back painful memories. Uncle Ramon had died several years before in a motorcycle wreck, landing almost at Aunt Sylvie's feet. To see someone else flying through the air to die . . .

Everyone watched silently as Dr. Fries arrived and checked Walt. He shook his head and stood up, and the group shifted uneasily. Raising his voice, the doctor called out to Sheriff McBride, "I'm afraid he's gone, Pete. You want to radio the hospital—have them send out the ambulance? Tell 'em no siren." The final instruction—*no siren*—caused a sigh to pass over the group like a sudden gust of wind. There was no need for a siren; Walt was beyond help.

Sam felt someone take her elbow from behind and turned. Tim's face was gray behind the tan. He had been standing off to one side, alone. "I was supposed to ride that horse." His voice was low and unsteady. "I almost did."

The next morning after breakfast, Sam went out on the porch. She needed to spend some time by herself and sort out what had been going on. After Tim had left the rodeo, Sam had found herself lost in the middle of a group of family and friends, including Paul. Everyone was in shock. Even so, speculation and rumors about Walt's accident had already begun.

"I've heard of freak accidents," Mick had said. "But they always just seemed like stories. Nothing like this has ever happened to anyone I know."

"I don't think it was an accident," Sam said, looking directly at Paul. "Tim was supposed to be riding that horse."

"I guess Tim was lucky," Nicole said.

"You think someone is out to get Tim?" Mick asked.

"I don't know." Sam sighed. "It just seems like too many things have happened for it all to be coincidence. If Aunt Sylvie hadn't stopped Tim, he would have . . ."

"Died," Paul interrupted. "And Walt would still be here."

Sam couldn't believe that Paul had said that. But Paul was surprising her a lot lately. She hoped that he was just being jealous, but in the back of her mind she couldn't help thinking that Paul might be responsible for Walt's death.

Filming resumed Monday morning amid mutters about bad luck. John juggled the schedule enough to allow time for people to attend the funeral.

Sam still had a lot of questions about Walt's accident. The biggest ones had to do with the cinch. The buckle was broken. Even though it looked all right and it could be fastened, it wouldn't hold. Normally, whoever had saddled the horse would have checked it. So far, no one admitted being responsible. Anyone could have fastened the cinch in a hurry and neglected to check it. Walt could even have done it himself. Sam figured no one would ever know.

Walt's funeral was held on a dry, windy day. There was enough dust in the air to irritate a lot of eyes. That gave an excuse to many of the men who didn't like to be seen crying. The town, of course, turned out in strength for one of its young people so suddenly, tragically dead. The small Hollywood contingent sat together, not really part of the community. Nicole skipped it, telling Sam privately that funerals left her so depressed she couldn't work for weeks.

But John was there, and Tim and Mick, and all of the stunt riders. Even Dave made it, although Nicole told Sam he'd gone back into his shell after the accident. Stunt work and rodeos were both always dangerous; Sam could understand Dave not liking the ugly reminder. According to Nicole, some crew members had started calling *West Wind* an unlucky show. She claimed she wasn't superstitious, but she sounded so nervous when she said it Sam didn't believe her.

Sam wondered if there *was* some sort of jinx on the show. She asked John when he came by that evening after the funeral. He just laughed. "Sammie, show business people are the most superstitious in the world," he said. "There were a couple of accidents and people got spooked. Walt's accident had nothing to do with the movie." Sam wasn't convinced, and she wasn't sure John believed his own comforting words. He didn't mention that Tim had almost taken that ride.

With the funeral behind them, filming got underway again. The scene they were shooting reminded everyone of the ill-fated Fourth of July rodeo. Jeb, Tim's character, had to compete with his best friend Lenny, played by Mick. The scene portrayed a climax to the rivalry that had been poisoning their friendship. Naturally, that meant it was the biggest rodeo of the year. Once the comparison had been made between the cinematic rodeo and the real one, the image stuck.

Two days after the funeral, Sam, her dad, and Aunt Sylvie watched some filming at John's invitation. Sam's mom declined, stating with a grin that if she had some extra time, she wanted to sit down and put her feet up. The three went over to the arena after lunch. Sam had already watched them filming several times, but her father hadn't. Sam suppressed a grin as Aunt Sylvie went straight over to join John. It was obvious why he'd invited them. Her father also appeared to know what was going on. He chuckled and told Sam, "About time Sis had a little fun again." He watched John and Sylvie talking for a moment, then turned to examine the arena.

The opening scene was an argument between Jeb and Lenny. It was the first time Sam had seen Tim since the Fourth, except at the funeral. He hadn't been visiting Worthless in the evenings. She wondered about it, but in a way she was glad. She needed time to sort out how she felt about him.

They watched as Tim and Mick got ready to film the sequence. The actors stood as though frozen in place. Larry Cabot called, "I'd like it very quiet, please." Several people echoed him loudly, calling "Quiet!" People around the set stopped talking and moving. John said, "Roll, please." Again there was an echo, "Rolling!" As Larry said, "Marker," a man stepped forward with the clapper board, the hinged chalkboard Sam had seen in movies about movies. He held it in front of the camera, then slapped it closed. The sound would enable them to get the film and soundtrack synched. Finally, John called, "Action!"

Mick said, "Jeb, you really think you can beat me?" His expression was that of someone on the verge of losing it completely. Tim, teeth clenched, turned and stalked away. The camera dolly, a small wheeled platform, was pushed along silently by several men as the camera followed Tim. "Dammit, answer me!"

Tim whirled and said, "By the time this rodeo's over, you're gonna wish you never said one word about it." The dialogue continued as the grips holding large, shiny boards moved around, focusing reflected light on the pair.

Sam's father whispered, "What're those things?"

She grinned and said softly, "Shiny boards. *Shhh!*" Her dad gave her an indignant look.

A moment later, John called, "Cut!"

She added in a normal voice, "That's really what they're called! I asked Tim."

He laughed. "Logical, I suppose." Then, as the camera dolly was pushed back to its starting point and Tim and Mick walked back, he asked, "Now what?"

"Now they do it again," Sam said.

"Very quiet, please. . . . Quiet! Roll, please. . . . Rolling! Marker! Action!" Then Mick started, "Jeb, you really think . . ." and the same scene was filmed again. And again. And again.

By the fifth repetition, Jack Phillips's eyes were glazing over. "Why in hell do they keep doing the same part?"

Sam shrugged. "They always do. The first time I saw it, I decided acting's the most boring job in the world."

When John finally called for a halt, Tim said a

few words to him, then broke away and headed across the arena to the chutes. He spotted Sam and motioned for her to join him. With a muttered "Excuse me" to her father, she did. A calf was inside one of the pens, waiting to be released for the calf-roping segment. In the other section of the double chute, a saddled horse waited, obviously Tim's mount for the calf roping. It was one of several rodeo-trained horses that had been brought in from Tucson.

Tim smiled at her. "I've missed you."

"Uh . . . I guess we've both been busy."

"What's had you so busy?" he asked.

"I just wanted to think about some things," she said somberly. "Walt dying like that . . . I've never had a friend die before. I'd known him all my life."

"I've had friends die." Tim's face was bleak, and Sam's breath caught in her throat as she remembered his parents, dead in a plane crash years before. "You don't get used to it, but you learn to go on."

"Tim, I'm sorry." Sam spoke hesitantly, afraid of opening wounds again. "It's hard, sometimes, to connect you with the Tim Rafferty that's been in the news for so long. I knew about the . . ." She trailed off, then finished the phrase in a rush. "About the crash. I'm sorry."

Tim reached through the rails, rubbing the calf's head as if it were a dog. It responded in much the same fashion, swiping a broad pink tongue across his hand. Startled, he laughed, then turned back to Sam.

"Like I said, some things you don't get used to. Uncle Bill's been good to me—he was my guardian until I turned eighteen, Dad's younger brother—but I still miss them." He straightened up and smiled at her, the smile he seemed to reserve just for her.

"How're you going to work this?" Sam asked hurriedly, hoping to deflect any additional questions. Walt's death hadn't been the only thing keeping her away. "Can you rope a calf?"

For an answer, he took the lariat from the saddle and twirled the loop a bit. For the first few seconds, the ring of rope maintained its shape, then it crumpled in midair and flopped to the ground.

"I guess not," he admitted ruefully.

Sam grinned and took the rope. Without a word, she twirled it and sent it sailing to settle gently over a post. She pulled it taut with a quick jerk. The look on his face made her laugh.

"Wow." He grinned.

She shrugged, pleased. "Since you can't rope the calf yourself, how are they going to do the scene?"

"First they're going to film me riding out after the calf," he said. "Then Dave'll do a regular roping run. If he misses, they'll try again till he doesn't. Then I go out and take the rope. I think I can tie the calf. The idea is I'll do as much as I can, and they'll combine things."

Sam reclaimed the rope and looped it neatly, ready for use, back on the saddle horn. "It's a shame we can't have you do it instead of Dave," he said. "Just think of them trying to splice that together." A mischievous expression stole across his face as he said this, and he looked around the corner of the fence. Across the arena, John and Sylvie were talking, and Larry Cabot was talking to the cameraman.

"Maybe we can. Sam, have you ever done any calf-roping?"

"For competition, you mean, or just for fun? You saw my event. I'm a barrel racer." A smile danced across her face, as she realized what he had in mind. "I've done some roping for fun, though."

They didn't discuss it any further, just moved

81

as though they had rehearsed. Dave was coming toward them, but he wouldn't get there in time to stop a little joke. Sam mounted while Tim went around to the release mechanism. He hit it, sending the calf scampering out a second before the gate in front of the horse opened. Behind them, there was a shout from Dave and more yells across the arena as Larry and the cameraman spotted them. It was too late. With a yell, Sam dug in her heels, swinging the lariat. The loop snaked out and settled over the head of the fleeing calf. Sam grinned. She figured the toss was as much luck as skill. She wasn't going to argue it, though. She yanked the rope tight and pulled up; something was wrong.

Instead of coming to a stop and leaning back against the rope, the horse put his head down and tried to pitch Sam off. She grabbed the saddle horn with both hands. The lariat was awkward in her grip, and she risked turning loose long enough to throw it to one side. Sam hoped it was far enough; she didn't need to have the horse trip on it. Then she used both hands to hold on. This wasn't bronc riding, where she'd lose points if she didn't keep one hand clear. This was a horse going crazy beneath her. He reared and screamed, while Sam clung to his back. Then once more he was plunging head-first, back hooves kicking toward the sky. He jumped, traveling sideways, and even backed up. Sam couldn't control the maddened gelding. All she could do was hang on.

The end came suddenly. The horse reared, holding the pose for a moment like a statue, then dropped back to all fours for an instant before kicking his hind legs toward the sky again. The transition was too abrupt and Sam lost her grip. As she sailed through the air she heard a scream and a hoarse shout. Sam had time to think of Walt once before she hit.

She landed on one shoulder and tumbled forward in a sprawling somersault. For a moment she lay there, trying to make her lungs work. Tim got there as Sam struggled to sit up, with Aunt Sylvie and John just behind him. Her father brought up the rear, his face relaxing as she moved.

"Take it easy. Don't try to . . ." Tim stopped as she sat up the rest of the way. She sat there panting, tears stinging her eyes as the pain stabbed her shoulder. She felt herself trembling as the shock caught up with her.

"Sammie." Aunt Sylvie dropped beside her

and hugged her fiercely. "Oh, sugar, you're all right. I thought you were—"

"So did I," Tim said in a low voice.

Sam took a deep breath, then laughed shakily. "So did I, for a minute." Walt's name hung unspoken on the air.

"Being tossed off a horse isn't anything new," Sam's father said, banishing ghosts. "We're just," he paused, hunting for words, "just a little shook up about it right now."

"I think you'd better see a doctor and get checked out," John said behind her.

Tim pulled her to her feet. "John, I'm fine," Sam insisted. Her right shoulder was throbbing, but she was pretty sure it was just bruised and skinned.

Tim didn't release her hand. He stood close beside her now, holding on tightly. "Too far," she heard him mutter. "It's gone too far."

Late that night, Sam slipped out of the house for a few minutes. Her shoulder was too sore to sleep, and the events of the afternoon kept dancing through her brain.

Before she'd been able to ask Tim what he'd meant, the film's medic had arrived. He had taken Sam into a honey wagon, as the trailers with dressing rooms and rest rooms were called, and performed a fast examination. Her shoulder would be stiff for a couple of days, and she had some gravel rash from the landing, but other than that the fall had been more frightening than dangerous.

But it could have been dangerous. A wrangler from the crew captured the horse, which had calmed down as soon as Sam was off his back. It had been easy to figure out the reason for the gelding's fit: the curb chain was broken. The chain went under the horse's chin and kept the bridle in place. The stitches on the leather strap of this one had given way. When Sam had pulled back on the reins, the broken chain let the spade bit dig painfully into the roof of the horse's mouth. The fierce pain made the gelding go crazy.

Another accident. There had been so many since the movie company had arrived at the Lizardfoot. Tim's eye had almost been gouged out when the fence collapsed. Walt hadn't been part of the film, but he had ridden the horse that Tim was supposed to have been on, and he died.

Sam headed out to the scrap pile behind the hangar. The scraps from the arena construction had been tossed there. Maybe Sam could find something to explain the accidents plaguing *West Wind.*

The moon was only at first quarter, giving just enough light to show a figure moving around the hangar. Sam froze. Then, as the figure bent to look more closely at something, she recognized Tim. She switched on her flashlight and shone it toward him.

He straightened and whirled, the light in his hand stabbing out at her. "Sam! You scared me. What are you doing here?" He shifted the light so it no longer glared in her eyes and made his way back through the clutter.

"I could ask you the same thing," she said. "I live here, after all. What's your excuse?" One of the things that had kept her awake was wondering what Tim's role in all this was. She was sure she'd seen fear on his face more than once, and his comments that afternoon indicated he knew something about these accidents.

He panned the light across the scattered junk once more, then turned away. "I've been trying to find a reason for what's been going on around here. Maybe if I can figure out *how,* I'll be able to figure out *who.* It's no use, though. Three nights searching and I haven't found a thing."

"How do you know there's something to find?" Sam asked quietly. He said nothing for a few minutes, then took her arm.

"C'mon," he said. "Let's go to my trailer. I should have talked to you before this."

Sam felt self-conscious as he let her into the small structure. The narrow trailer had been divided in half, with two self-contained apartments. John Ryder had the other apartment and was probably asleep beyond the wall. Sam had been in the housing units a few times, leaving sodas and snacks, but always when no one was around. Now she was acutely aware of being alone with Tim in his apartment.

If Tim felt self-conscious, it didn't show. He motioned her to a seat on the tiny couch, and said, "Soda okay, or do you want some coffee?" She accepted a drink, then made room for him beside her.

As soon as he was seated, he started talking. "Being in show business is funny. I've done it all my life, and it's all I ever want to do, but there are drawbacks. Sometimes it's like you're a zoo animal living in a cage, watched all the time by everybody in the world. You get used to letters from people you'll never meet, who tell you things they haven't told their own families.

I've gotten love letters from girls almost since before I was old enough to read them, and if they rated letters the way they rate films, I'm still not old enough to read some of them. The decent ones I try to answer—the oddball ones I just throw away. That includes the ones that tell me I'm going to go to hell for acting, or because I don't follow some guru."

He took a deep breath. "I thought it was just another oddball letter, so I threw it away. Now I wish I hadn't."

"What letter?" The fear was there on his face again, not hidden now, and it was contagious.

"The letter I got telling me this was my last picture, that I was going to be killed before I hurt anyone else."

SEVEN

As she scrubbed pots and pans the next morning, Sam still felt fear forming a hard knot in her stomach. She and Tim had gone over all the accidents and foul-ups that had happened. Some were probably carelessness or honest accidents, especially the minor annoyances. Those could have been caused by tension, the way one slipup can lead to another. But some of them could have been deadly. And there was Walt.

"I don't believe it," Tim said when Sam tried to insist Walt's death had been an accident. "Everyone saw what was going on. Walt offered right away to let me take his ride. Someone asked him to do that. Then John stopped me, and it was too late to fix the cinch. Sure, the way he hit his head was a fluke, but what do you think would have happened if I'd been in the saddle? Walt was trying to get clear. I wouldn't have known how."

When Sam suggested he tell Sheriff McBride, Tim was reluctant. "What proof have I got? That's another problem with being an actor; everyone always thinks you're after free publicity. If I still had that letter . . . anyway, if I make too much of a fuss, the damned insurance company will shut us down. I need to finish this picture." Tim was taking a percentage of the film's box office receipts in exchange for a lower salary and had invested some of his own money as well.

She asked him what the letter meant about his hurting someone, and he was as puzzled by that as she was. It had to be some sort of imaginary hurt, he said. He'd never hurt anyone.

A faraway echo of Nicole's warnings sounded in Sam's mind as he said that—of the reputation Tim had for loving and leaving. That couldn't be the sort of thing the letter meant—or could it?

The broken curb chain had been the last straw. Watching Sam sailing through the air like Walt had scared him badly. As he said this, Tim had wrapped her in his arms. Sam's face grew hot as she remembered what followed. It had been quite late when she'd slipped back into the house and gone to bed.

"Sammie? Are you asleep with your eyes open?"

She came to with a start. Aunt Sylvie had gone out several minutes earlier with one of the big plastic tubs of scraps. Now Sylvie was staring at Sam quizzically, the merest trace of a smile on her face. Sam realized she'd been scrubbing on the same skillet for at least five minutes.

"Sorry, Aunt Sylvie. I was just thinking."

"'Bout what? Or should I ask, about who?" The wisp of a smile broadened into a grin as Sam hurried to rinse the pan, her face growing still hotter. Sam didn't blush, but sometimes she felt as though she did. This was one of those times.

Sam reached for another pan and tried to change the subject. "How'd all these pans get dirty at once? Mom usually gets them done before bed."

Her aunt chuckled. "I've been doing them, but last night I got in a little late. So'd someone else. I was still awake when you came in, Sam." She turned serious. "Maybe I shouldn't say anything. I'm in love myself, and it's a wonderful feeling."

Sam reached for the steel wool and scrubbed savagely at some dried sauce, not answering. Her shoulder was still sore and it ached as she applied pressure. After a moment, Sylvie sighed.

"Sam, I like Tim. He's good-looking, and he could charm the rattles off a snake. I can't blame you a bit for falling for him. Just don't let yourself get hurt. He's got a reputation for falling in and out of love about as often as some guys change their socks. And you're already national news."

Sam looked up from the saucepan in her hands. "Didn't anyone tell you?" Aunt Sylvie asked. "Hang on—let me get something." With that, the older woman left the room, leaving Sam to wonder what she'd meant.

A few minutes later, Sylvie returned with an open magazine and handed it to her. It was a cheap Hollywood gossip sheet. "Alice down at the post office told me about this," Sylvie said. "I showed John. He said this sort of thing always hits the gossip columns sooner or later and not to get upset, but I thought you should know." She pointed. The article was headed

"Who and Who," and was filled with tiny type and names in bold print. Halfway down the left column, Tim's name jumped out at her.

"Handsome Tim Rafferty has made another on-location conquest. His romance with a local beauty in the tiny town where his latest film is being made has set tongues to wagging. Is she destined to be left behind, like so many before her? Well, when Hollywood comes to town, hearts will break!"

There was more, but Sam couldn't face it.

Sylvie reclaimed the magazine, pulling it from Sam's limp fingers. "I thought it would be better for you to know about it. I don't know where these things get their information, but you can't keep something like this quiet. Not with someone as well known as Tim."

"How about you and John?" Sam asked bitterly. "I notice you two aren't in this thing."

Sylvie shook her head, untroubled. "We talked it over, and if they print anything about us, we'll just ignore it. Don't be mad at me, Sammie. Go ahead and have fun with Tim. Only . . . keep it just fun."

Sam wiped her hands on her apron. "We need to put out sodas." She got out the ice chest and they headed for the trailers, carrying the awkward load between them.

The magazine article left Sam feeling horribly exposed, almost as though she was walking around naked. She wondered if Tim had seen it. He might be used to such things, but it bothered her. And sooner or later someone was bound to show the article to Paul. That meant trouble—big trouble.

They turned down the alley between the two rows of trailers. The one used by Tim and John was next to them. Sam stumbled slightly as she tripped over something on the path. A shadow shifted and there was a metallic creak; then, Sylvie shoved her hard.

"Look out!"

Sam half jumped, half fell forward, dropping her end of the ice chest. As she landed on her knees, a huge light fell with a crash. Bits of metal and wire flew, as it exploded on impact. Sam's arm stung. A shard of glass had scratched her skin. Pain shot through her arm. She looked down and saw blood seeping through her torn shirt.

Beside her, Aunt Sylvie was sprawled in a twisted mass of metal and glass.

"Aunt Sylvie!" Sam shrieked. "Are you all

right?" Aunt Sylvie pushed herself to a sitting position.

She grimaced slightly and shook her head. "I don't know, but I think I busted my ankle," Aunt Sylvie said. There was a shout, and Tim and several others ran toward them. They gathered around, asking questions. Tim dropped to his knees beside Sam.

"What happened? What's that light doing here?" John Ryder pushed his way to the front. He wasn't asking questions so much as demanding answers. There was silence for a moment.

"Is that a light?" Sylvie looked at the shards of glass with distaste. "Doesn't look like one now. Sam tripped on a cable and that—*thing*—started to fall on us. We jumped. It didn't even brush me, but I landed wrong. My ankle's messed up." The joint was already swollen.

"It's a twelve-K light," Tim said. "We use it for night work." Sam had seen some of them, although so far there had been no filming after dark. But lights were stored in the locked equipment trailer—not left out between the housing units.

John Ryder stooped and gently touched Aunt Sylvie's swollen ankle. "That looks bad, Sylvie.

We were lucky that light didn't land on you. They're surprisingly heavy."

"Ow." She flinched at the delicate touch. "Yeah, it hurts." She managed a smile that was no more than half grimace. "I think I'm going to need some help getting back to the house."

"Of course." Carefully, he helped her get up, making sure the weight was on her good foot. Then, her arm around his neck and his around her waist, they started slowly toward the house.

Tim took Sam's hand. "Are you all right? There's blood on your arm." He wiped it off gently with his fingers. The bleeding was already stopping.

"Just a scratch," Sam said. Her voice was shaky. Now that the crisis was over, she realized how close it had been. "I think a piece of glass hit it."

"That's my trailer," Tim said. His voice was shaking. "That light was meant for me."

Late that afternoon, Sam got to the arena just as John called, "All right, that's a wrap. Thank you very much," signaling the end of the day's shooting. The second AD handed out the call sheets, which told everyone on the set what time they had to be where for the next day's shooting. Mick spotted her and came over.

"Well, the trick rider," Mick greeted her with a grin. His blue eyes, which Sam had heard Jackie call "mad Irish," danced as he added, "I hope you won't pull that particular trick often."

"Don't worry, I don't intend to," Sam said. "My shoulder's still sore."

"Tell Tim to watch how he holds you, then." Sam scowled, and he added quickly, "What's the matter—you two have a fight?"

"No," Sam admitted. "I'm just wondering how everyone knows so much about my business all of a sudden!"

"Ah. I forgot this is your first time being caught in the rumor mills. You get used to it." Mick gave her a twisted smile and went on. "Maybe I should say you almost get used to it. I just wonder what Jackie will say when it happens to us."

"Jackie?" Sam hadn't thought of that. "I mean, I knew you were dating her, but . . ." She floundered to a stop.

"Dating, yeah. She's special, Sam. Of course, you've known her all your life—you know how sweet she is. I'm afraid the Hollywood news treatment is going to be a real shock to her."

Sam looked at him doubtfully. *Sweet* wasn't a word she'd use about Jackie, and Sam didn't think she'd be upset about being linked publicly to Mick. But Sam kept her mouth firmly shut. If Mick was in love with Jackie, he wouldn't want to hear anything against her. Maybe she wasn't so bad. Still, Sam wasn't quite ready to start a Jackie McBride fan club.

Mick grew serious. "Sammie, I know Jackie's a little young for me—hell, neither one of you's out of high school—but I think this is for real. I'm glad you two are friends."

This sure was the summer for romance, Sam thought. She was pretty positive Aunt Sylvie and John were looking at marriage, and now Mick was talking like this. "I hope it works out," Sam told him. She kept her doubts to herself.

"It will." He grinned, mad Irish eyes sparkling. "I've made up my mind, so that settles it."

Tim finished his discussion with John and the assistant directors and came over. "How's your aunt?" he asked.

"Her aunt?" Mick raised an eyebrow.

Sam bit her lip as Tim said, "One of the twelve-K's almost fell on them this morning.

Over by my trailer. They jumped clear, but Sylvie hurt her ankle."

Mick let out a whistle. "Not just trick riding, stunt work as well. Why didn't you say something, Sammie?"

She shrugged. "She's all right. Dad took her in for an X ray. It's just a sprain, not a break. They've got her in an air cast." The inflated brace would support and protect the joint while it healed.

"What the hell was a twelve-K doing over *there*?" Mick asked. There was no trace of a smile on his face.

"Larry's trying to find that out," Tim said.

"It was just an accident." Sam tried to sound nonchalant.

"Yeah. Another one." Tim's voice was bitter. From the look on his face, Sam was sure he was thinking about the letter. A few minutes later, Mick left. He was rooming at a bed and breakfast located next door to the McBrides' sprawling house. As soon as he was gone, Tim put an arm around Sam's waist. Since there were at least a dozen people within view, it made her uncomfortable. Any one of the people working around them could have been responsible for the article. Quick to notice her lack of response, Tim asked, "What's wrong?"

Sam said, "Nothing serious, but can we go someplace and talk? Someplace without an audience?"

"Let's go for a ride in my Bronco," he suggested. "You can show me some more of the ranch, and we can talk all you want."

They drove north from headquarters, following the rough dirt road up Lizardfoot Canyon. As they bounced over the washboard surface, Sam told Tim about the article. His lips tightened slightly as she quoted the final line.

" 'So many before her'? They must think I've got a record like Don Juan! Sam, I'm sorry, but there's nothing I can do about those buzzards. Just try to ignore it."

"Don't insult buzzards that way. At least they wait until the meat's dead." Sam meant it as a joke, but it came out with too much heat.

She felt out of control when she was with Tim. Like she was floating down a river, heading right for a waterfall. She'd have to figure out where their relationship was headed later on. Right then she wanted to enjoy floating.

"Who comes out this way?" Tim asked as they turned up a steep side road. The new road, more a rough track than a road, climbed the side of the canyon.

"It's all private, but sometimes the BLM people come out." He looked blank, and she added, "Bureau of Land Management. We own only a part of our land. We lease the rest from the government. Most ranches are like that." Sam pointed back toward the road they'd left, now some distance beneath them. "Mainly, we use the road to haul cattle or salt blocks, fence posts, whatever. But we don't bother trying to keep it maintained."

The right front tire dropped into a bone-jarring hole as she spoke. She grabbed the dash as they bounced over it, and Tim's grip on the wheel tightened. "You're joking. This is a great road. Great like a cheese grater." They hit another hole as Sam laughed, and the jolt almost made her bite her tongue.

The track leveled out short of the top, and Sam had Tim stop. "Now, look down on the canyon floor," she directed. She pointed to small groups of cattle, scattered throughout the area they'd just come through. Tim sighted along her arm. There were dozens of animals. Some were in small washes, some hidden by a fold of land or a clump of mesquite.

After a while, they got ready to drive on. "Over the top, or back the way we came?" Tim asked.

"There's a spot that's wide enough to turn around about a half-mile farther up."

They reached the wide spot, and Tim cautiously turned the vehicle. There wasn't much room for error—the ground fell away steeply a few inches beyond the road. Once he had reversed the Bronco, Tim killed the engine and unfastened his seat belt.

He set the emergency brake, then slid awkwardly across the floor console between the seats. "These things aren't designed for this," he muttered, bumping against the steering wheel. She couldn't help laughing at that, even as her breath grew short. She released her own seat belt and turned to him. His arms were waiting.

The kiss was gentle at first, then grew warmer, her pulse growing faster. Finally, after an unmeasured time, Tim moved his head back a few inches. His fingers combed her sun-streaked hair. "Your eyes are green today," he whispered. Sam's eyes were the shade of hazel that shifted color with the light and her mood.

"That means I'm happy," she said, smiling at

him. His hand slipped down from her hair and gently touched her shoulder. Gentle or not, it was the sore one and she flinched. Tim snatched his hand back.

"I'm sorry," he said.

"It's fine." Sam wasn't ready for the magic to end. But it had. Tim slid back into the driver's seat. After a moment, Sam fastened her seat belt and Tim started the engine. Sam's painful shoulder was a souvenir of the accidents. The reminder destroyed the mood for both of them.

Tim started the engine and turned on the headlights as the sun dropped below the opposite wall of Lizardfoot Canyon. They were halfway down the track on a long steep grade, when they started picking up speed. Sam's grip on the dash handle tightened. There was a switchback ahead. She opened her mouth to speak, but the words died when she looked at Tim's set face. He was pumping the brake pedal furiously. His face white, he shouted, "No brakes!" just as they came to the first curve of the switchback.

Tim wrenched the wheel around, trying to follow the sharp curve, but it was impossible. They went over the edge, dropping down an almost vertical slope. Tim straightened the wheel quickly, to keep them from rolling. If they rolled, the roof would be crushed. The twisting road was only a dozen feet below them, but the vehicle had too much momentum. It slid down onto the road, and across, and back off the road, heading for the canyon floor.

Sam's teeth ached with the effort of not screaming, as Tim wrestled with the steering wheel. He wasn't wasting effort pumping the useless brakes. The emergency brake might work, but it could flip them. If they started rolling, they'd be dead. Sam's eyes shut involuntarily, as a thick-trunked scrub oak loomed before them in the dusk. Then she forced her eyes open. No matter what, she'd rather see what happened. They skidded to one side of the tree as Tim fought the wheel. There was a crunch as the rear left side of the Bronco side-swiped the tree.

Trees and brush whipped past. They hit one large rock with a clang that could be heard for miles. Sam stopped breathing as a high bounce nearly turned them over, but they landed back on their wheels with a heavy thud and continued down, skidding on the now-flattened tires.

The slope grew less steep as they approached the bottom. Finally, they slid sideways into another tree, this one a rock-solid mesquite. They bounced off it and skidded partway over a spur of rock. The Bronco came to rest at an angle, its right wheels off the ground over an additional drop.

EIGHT

The nightmare ride was over. They sat frozen for a moment; then Tim said, "We made it," in a flat voice. The engine had died when they slammed into the final rock. Now Tim reached forward to switch off the key.

Everything had happened so quickly. Only minutes had passed since Tim had realized something was wrong. Tim unfastened his seat belt slowly, moving like an old man, as Sam leaned back against the headrest of her seat, the tremors in her body increasing to a violent shaking. She shut her eyes, then opened them in sudden panic, as images from the long descent played back against her closed eyelids. It felt as though they were moving.

Tim reached over and gently brushed away her tears. Sam hadn't even noticed she was crying until that point. "We'd better get out," he said. "Can you slide over to my side? I don't think you can get out on yours."

Carefully, they both slid out the driver's door. The vehicle rocked dangerously as they moved. Once they were out, they scrambled a little way up the hillside and looked at the ruined Bronco. "They named that thing for the wrong animal," Tim said. "It came down this hill like a cat."

Sam looked back up the steep slope. "You set a speed record for coming down the mountain, Tim. Only next time, I think I'd rather walk." Sam fought down hysterical giggles, the tension beginning to dissipate. They were alive—that was all that mattered.

The light was fading fast now in the narrow canyon and they were a long way from the ranch headquarters. There was no way the Bronco was going to move under its own power. Tim walked over and gingerly climbed back inside the unstable wreck, long enough to retrieve his flashlight from under the driver's seat. He rejoined Sam with it in hand.

"Any idea how far we're going to have to hike?" he asked.

She looked around for landmarks. After a moment, she got her bearings.

"Let's get back to the road while there's still a little light," she said. "That'll be the roughest part. The road will lead us home. It's about six miles."

By the time they got back to the dusty, well-packed road, the last daylight had faded. Stars were thick overhead, but they didn't offer much light for hiking, and it would be hours before the moon cleared the canyon walls.

It took almost two hours for them to get back to the ranch headquarters. While neither one of them was wearing hiking boots, Sam was in better shape than Tim. She had on her sneakers, while he was in his riding boots. The high-heeled boots had never been intended for walking any distance, and he was limping before they'd covered the first mile. They slowed almost to a crawl and stopped as often as they could.

When they finally emerged from the mouth of the canyon and saw the lights of home, tears once more slipped quietly down Sam's face.

During the harrowing ride down the mountainside, she'd been too scared to think, but she'd come too close to seeing the familiar ranch house never again. Now that it was in view, she knew how much she really loved it. It was old-fashioned and it needed a new coat of paint, but it was home. They headed for the lights, Tim now leaning on her as the pain in his feet grew worse.

Sam hoped they'd be able to slip into the ranch house quietly, but their luck had evaporated with the safe descent. As she opened the kitchen door, voices drifted out from the main room: her parents, Aunt Sylvie, and John.

Mrs. Phillips came into the kitchen to investigate the noise. "Sam! Where have you been all evening?" Catching sight of Tim, she added dryly, "Hello, Tim. Where have you *both* been?"

"We went out for a drive, and we had a little trouble—" Sam began, just as her mother got a better look at Sam's tear-streaked face and Tim's limp.

"What on earth happened?" she demanded. Without giving Sam a chance to respond, she called, "Jack!"

"What is it, Marion?" He hurried toward

them as she urged Sam and Tim into the living room. They dropped onto the couch exhausted. With an exclamation of dismay, John and Sylvie joined them. Tim groaned with relief as he got the weight off his feet. He took off his boots as John stood over them, insisting on an immediate explanation.

"Like I said, we went for a drive," Sam started once more. Her face felt gritty and it struck her how tattered they must both look.

"Sam." Jack Phillips's voice was quiet. "You know the rules. We let you have a lot of freedom, but you're supposed to let us know when you go someplace."

Tim took over. "We went out in my Bronco, Mr. Phillips. We drove up the canyon for a while; then we took this steep side road."

"The Spider Walk, Dad," Sam added.

Tim was diverted from his story for a moment. "You didn't tell me it was called that. Good name for it. Anyway, we turned around up there and headed back down just after sunset, and the brakes went out."

"What?" Everyone spoke at once.

"We just sort of slid down the mountain," Tim said quickly. "The Bronco's a wreck. It'll take a truck to move it. We had to walk out."

Tim had gingerly pulled his socks off as he spoke, and now he wiggled his toes. "And it took us a long time because of this."

Sylvie went off to get some dry bandages. Jack had Tim describe the damage to the Bronco and the location so he could haul it out. Sam lay back against the soft leather of the sofa, savoring the feeling of warmth and security.

She felt eyes on her and opened her own. John Ryder was staring at her and Tim both, a troubled expression on his face. Sam couldn't blame him. Another accident. And this one had nearly killed both of them.

Tim was upset that despite his effort to downplay the crash, word of the incident spread quickly. Several crew members went out the next day with Jack Phillips to winch the Bronco out and haul it to Agua Verde and the local garage. By the next evening, half the people in town had driven by the Green Water Garage to look at the wrecked vehicle. Late that afternoon, a news crew arrived from Tucson. They drove out to the ranch and cornered John in the production office.

Tim found out about it when John showed up on the set with the reporters. They filmed a brief interview with him for the news that evening. He went over to the ranch house to watch it with the Phillipses and John. It hadn't gone too badly, he thought, watching himself. He'd seen his face so many times on the screen that it was like watching a stranger. He could judge his performance from a distance. And it had been a performance. He examined his own image critically. No, there was no trace of residual fear there.

"We were lucky, of course," Tim was saying modestly on the television screen. "But it wasn't that bad. No, the authorities aren't investigating the accident. There's nothing to investigate." Tim frowned as the picture on the screen shifted to a shot of the totaled Bronco, while the voice-over described the damages. Without contradicting Tim directly, the impression was left of a close brush with death and a cover-up.

Tim wasn't really sure what McBride thought about the accident. He knew they were going over the wreckage carefully down at the garage. Tim hadn't told the sheriff about the letter, and he had no intentions of doing so.

"Looks pretty good," John said as Jack Phillips flipped off the set. "I don't think it will get too much play, and I doubt if there'll be any bad publicity out of it."

"There's no such thing as bad publicity, John," Tim remarked. That was an old show business saying. "It'll probably help."

John shook his head obstinately. "Yeah, I know that's what they say. But I also know that bad publicity can kill you."

Tim didn't agree. There had been movies in the past that had seen numerous deaths—not just near-misses—and they hadn't suffered at the box office for it. He suspected John just didn't want a reputation for directing films that were jinxed. And right now, *West Wind* was definitely a bad luck show.

The accident had scared Tim much more than the interview showed. He'd watched stunt men do similar tricks many times, but he'd never forget the terror he'd felt when they slipped over the edge. At least Sam hadn't been hurt.

He swore to himself that, no matter what, Sam wouldn't be hurt.

Two days after the wreck, a crowd of Agua Verdeans arrived at the ranch early in the morning. The final scenes for the rodeo sequence were to be shot with the extras hired from town. There had been a brief meeting with the potential extras a week before. The second AD, who was acting as extras coordinator, had given them simple instructions. None of them would be seen closely enough on screen to need professional make-up, and clothing would be whatever they would normally wear to attend a rodeo. All they were there for, he told them, was to "decorate the set."

The one extra who could be spotted easily was Mindy. To her delight, her bulky white cast was considered a good touch. She was assigned a place in the front where she was to prop the cast up so it would be visible. Sam remembered the last rodeo they'd all been at together. Walt's absence was carefully not mentioned by anyone. It was still too painful.

At Tim's urging, the Phillipses had signed up to be in the movie. When they got to the small grandstand by the arena, Sam was amazed. It looked as though most of Agua Verde had the film bug. Jackie was there, of course, a possessive hand on Mick's arm. He was no longer considered an outsider by most of the townspeople, partly because of Jackie and partly because everybody liked him. The couple stood at the center of a group of people who were all cracking up at one of Mick's jokes. Jackie waved to Sam and she joined them. Sam wasn't sure how deep the change in Jackie went. She was a lot happier than Sam had ever seen her in the past. Mick had been good for her.

The old Jackie hadn't disappeared completely, though. She pulled Sam to one side and asked, "Did you hear what the news said about the accident?" Sam shook her head and Jackie continued. "Some people are saying the whole thing was a fake, just to get publicity for the film. There's supposed to be a car wreck in the film, you know. They said Tim's Bronco was rigged so it would be just like the accident in the film."

Sam was furious. She'd had nightmares about that hell-ride down the mountain. "That's ridiculous and you know it! Who's been spreading that manure?"

Jackie shrugged. "I just heard it around. Someone at the garage said all the brake lines were leaking or loose, something like that. I'll bet it shows up in 'Who and Who,' though."

At the mention of the column, Sam's fist clenched at her side. Thanks to Mick, Jackie knew all the gossip around the production these days. So far the scandalmongers hadn't said a word about Mick O'Connell. Maybe Jackie was supplying the local view? Sam considered the idea, until Jackie spoke again.

"I wonder if Paul really is going to deck Tim," Jackie said.

"What?"

"Paul's here today. Down at the café yesterday, Chet asked him why you were with Tim when he had the accident." Jackie's eyes were bright with interest. "And Paul said he didn't know, but he was going to knock Tim clear back to California for almost getting you killed. Only, I don't think that's the only reason."

"Paul's here?" Sam refused to respond to the rest. "I thought he wasn't going to have anything to do with this circus, as he called it."

Jackie pointed. Paul was standing behind the grandstand alone. "I don't know if he's signed up as an extra or not, but he's here all right."

When Sam joined Paul a few minutes later, he didn't say anything at first. Only after she greeted him did he say, "Hey, Sammie." Then silence again. She'd have to start the conversation if she wanted one.

"I thought you didn't want to be in this," she said.

"I don't." He stopped and stared into the distance again.

Sam had been avoiding Paul and she knew it. She had mixed feelings about him. He'd always been close to her, but Tim made her feel special. And she didn't like Paul's jealousy. Sam couldn't help remembering that Paul had been the main one egging Tim on, daring him to try a bronc ride. She'd asked Tim if he thought Paul had caused the accidents.

"He probably wouldn't cry if I got myself busted up," Tim had answered. "But I don't think he'd actually do anything. Why would he have sent me that letter? The letter has something to do with it—I know it does." He'd kissed her, warm and long, then added, "I sure can't blame him for hating me. I should hate him for finding you first."

Sam was about to give up on Paul when he spoke again. "I came out to see you," he said. "Wanted to see if you were okay."

"I'm fine," she said. She knew there was more to it than that.

Now he looked at her straight-on for the first time. "I haven't seen much of you lately. Like you've been avoiding me. Or maybe you've been too busy going out with him."

Sam could hear the question Paul hadn't asked: Which one of them was she in love with? She had no answer. She looked at the face she knew as well as her own. The short sandy hair was completely unlike the soft fall of Tim's blond hair. Paul's eyes were brown and Tim's were a blinding blue. Despite the differences, Paul's face was as attractive as Tim's—and as strong. And his chin was just as stubborn.

"They'll be done with the movie in a couple more weeks," she said. It wasn't an answer.

"They'll leave, yeah. But I'm not so sure that'll solve things." With a muttered "See you later," he left.

"See you," she said faintly to his back. She spoke too late; he hadn't heard. Biting her lip, she started back to the stands. These days life was full of questions, she thought. The deadly question of who was responsible for the accidents was the most urgent. She focused on the letter. It had to be connected. Tim was right about Paul. He couldn't have sent the letter. There was no reason for Paul to have threatened Tim prior to the actor's arrival at the ranch. Tim hadn't even met Sam yet.

Sam's attention was so far away, she didn't see Helen until she almost knocked her down.

"Sorry, Helen, I wasn't watching where I was going," Sam apologized. She liked Helen's outfit, an elaborate rodeo costume. It was a duplicate of the one Sam had seen Nicole wearing earlier.

"Are you an extra? You'd better get around front." Helen looked at the camera platform across the arena and added, "I think they're about ready to start. They're doing Tim's scene with Nicole first, then the one with the rodeo clowns."

"When do you go out?" Sam asked, curious.

"Not till they're done with the stars," Helen said. "They're going to film the whole thing with them faking the stunt; then we go in and they turn the bull loose. I think John planned it that way so they wouldn't have to worry about losing time if the bull wouldn't cooperate." She grinned.

As if to underline her words, there was a bellow from the pen farthest from the camera platform, where a massive Brahma bull waited for his chance to perform. Tim had described the scene to her. It was wildly improbable, since in real life there were no such things as female rodeo clowns. But the script described Amy, Nicole's character, as a rebel who managed to

120

defy the conventions and win a place as a clown.

Sam's attention wandered as Tim crossed to the platform to speak with John. Helen's voice beside her was quiet. "You're really hooked on him, aren't you?"

Sam's laugh was rueful as she turned back to the stunt rider. "It shows that much? Yeah, I guess I am."

"I hope you don't wind up regretting it," Helen said, her voice pitched so low Sam wasn't sure the words were meant for her. Before she could ask Helen to explain, the second AD came around the end of the grandstand.

"There you are!" he exclaimed. "Mr. Ryder asked me to find you. They need you and Dave over with the clowns, and I have to get back to my extras." He frowned at Sam. "Extras are supposed to be seated by now, Miss Phillips. Where's Dave?" Helen pointed in the general direction of the pens and he headed that way, calling over his shoulder to Helen, "They're waiting."

"I'd better go," she told Sam.

Sam followed slowly. It was bad enough trying to decide how she felt about Tim without all these hints. Tim was an actor, which meant he was automatically suspect as far as most people were concerned. Sam didn't intend to jump to that conclusion, but a lot of other people seemed willing to.

Sam had just sat down next to her parents when the clapper board was slapped. "Action!" John called. In the arena, Tim sprinted across the dirt to grab Nicole. They argued. Sam couldn't hear the dialogue, but she knew it was about Amy's intention to try to sneak into the ring as a clown. The mike, covered with what looked like a fuzzy sock to cut wind noise, was close enough to pick up the voices, but the extras were too far away to hear. Behind the actors, other members of the stunt team rode in and out of camera range in a carefully planned pattern, forming an action backdrop that included the stands. Mindy was in the center of the front row, cast prominent. *It might be possible for Mindy to see herself in the finished movie,* Sam thought. *That is, if she examined one frame at a time with a magnifying glass.*

The filming continued. As always, Sam was startled by how much time was spent setting up shots. The argument between Amy and Jeb was repeated six times before John was satisfied.

The next scene would start with Lenny,

played by Mick, injured. Jeb would be thrown from his horse while picking him up, and Nicole as Amy would jump into the arena, closer to the bull than the clowns, and lure the animal away. Sam could think of a dozen things wrong with the scene, but she'd admitted to Tim when he'd described it to her earlier that it would be exciting. Sam guessed that excitement counted more than accuracy sometimes in movies.

John planned to film the entire scene with the three actors first. There would be some shots of the stands, giving the extras their one chance at acting. They were told to react to the pretend situation with horror and alarm. They were also warned, "No cheering or laughing!" There was a wave of suppressed giggles at this, naturally. It would be hard to react to imaginary danger. After the scene was completed, they would film it again with the stunt doubles and the bull.

The cameras rolled for the first part of the scene. Tim rode out and the clowns moved around in the background, luring off the imaginary bull. Sam had seen this pair of clowns in a professional rodeo once, but she wasn't sure from a distance which was which. The cameras stopped, and Tim dismounted.

Later, Dave would fake being thrown. Tim sprawled on the ground as though he had been thrown there, rolling around a little to get his clothes dusty. The make-up man added a few more artistic smudges of dust, then went back to the side. Tim held his position, waiting for the call of "Action," when Nicole screamed, a genuine scream of terror. Tim raised his head and froze.

Forty feet away from him, the gate on the pen had swung open. The Brahma, more than a ton of angry bull, came out and stopped, his head swinging from side to side. Behind Tim the horse that had supposedly thrown him neighed and galloped to the other end of the arena. Sam rose to her feet in horror, as grips and lighting people scrambled for the fences. One of the wranglers grabbed Tim's horse. People around Sam were on their feet now as well. Her mother put an arm around Sam's shoulders as she clenched her hands, powerless to do anything but watch.

Tim rose halfway to his feet, then froze again in a crouch as the bull took a few more steps toward him. The Brahma tossed his head, his wide nostrils testing the wind. Tim was too close—if he tried to run for it, the bull would overtake him before he was halfway to the nearest fence. An uncanny hush fell over the small arena as they waited for the bull's next move. It took a few more steps, shaking its head, then trotted straight toward Tim, picking up speed as it went.

With a long, high-pitched whoop, one of the clowns ran up from the far end of the arena. He paused near Tim and the bull, and the Brahma stopped in its tracks, confused by the noisy newcomer. The other clown came up behind him, stopping by one of the safety barrels. The first clown waved a scarf at the bull and called while the other ran toward the bull, then back to the barrel, then toward him again. The animal took another step in Tim's direction.

Sam bit her tongue to keep from screaming. She'd seen what a bull had done once to a horse, and that bull hadn't been half the size of this Brahma. The long, wickedly hooked horns lowered toward Tim, and Sam stopped breathing.

She let out the pent-up air with an unconsciously labored sigh, as the bull stopped again. The massive head turned curiously toward one of the clowns, who had let out a coyote yip. In the silence covering the rest of the arena, the calm voice of the other clown could be heard clearly. "Kid, when I give the word, you run like hell. But not till I give the word." Then he pranced in place, waggling his fingers alongside his head like horns. *"Heeey, bully-bully-bull!"*

With a bellow, the bull turned and headed for the foolish creature who was annoying him. His speed was terrifying. The clown ducked behind the barrel and the bull stopped, confused. His partner got on the other side of the beast and called again. The bull made a short dash at his second tormenter, who ducked again, while the first moved a little farther away, luring the animal still farther from Tim.

The deadly dance continued for several minutes. At one point, one of the men had to scramble into the barrel, and the bull knocked it over, but the other drew him off again.

Finally, one of the clowns got behind the bull. They had worked the angry animal over until they were close to the side. He called out, "Okay, kid, hit the fence!" As he said it, he slapped the bull on the rump. The bull twisted around, searching for his antagonist as he ducked behind the barrel, then scrambled over the fence.

On the other side of the arena, Tim broke

126

from his crouch into a sprint. He reached the fence and almost threw himself over it. The Brahma slammed into the fence after him, frustrated but in sole possession of the arena.

Filming was over for the day.

NINE

No one could figure out how the gate had opened. Sheriff McBride, who had been there as an extra, examined it, and nothing seemed to be wrong. They finished filming the scene the next day with no further problems. The two clowns accepted Tim's thanks but were uneasy at the fuss being made over them. They refused John's offer to arrange press interviews and left right after the filming. It had been the finest example Sam had ever seen of the art of a rodeo clown. And she hoped she'd never see anything like it again.

The following morning the trucks were loaded with equipment, as most of the production headed out for several days of remote location work. While most of the action in the film was set close to the ranch house, John wanted to include the spectacular view from Lizard Peak. The setting was a large part of why he'd chosen the Lizardfoot in the first place. The honey wagons, generators, and electrical trucks were hauled halfway up the mountain to a plateau overlooking the Agua Verde Valley. The rugged terrain rising beyond Lee's Flat to the peak would be a perfect setting for several major scenes.

Shifting the movie's base of operations fifteen miles up a dirt road was less trouble than Sam had expected. The road saw more traffic than it had in the past fifty years, and a haze of dust hung in the air for almost an hour at times, causing some problems for the cameras. Jack Phillips was worried about what would happen once the rains came. If they didn't get all that equipment off the mountain before then, the rough road would turn into a bog. But there were few other problems. Sam took turns with her aunt and mother driving up the mountain with the food and reheating it on the site. Twice a day the ranch truck bounced over the ruts, which were growing deeper and deeper with the increased traffic.

After the wreck in the Bronco, Tim had resumed his evening visits with Sam to see Worthless. They'd even managed to go riding a couple of times. Now the walks were curtailed again, as filming lasted from morning until late into the night. The brief time they had together was spent discussing the accidents—over and over. Tim had asked Dave if anyone had been around the bull's pen that day, but the stunt man hadn't seen anything. The broken latch on the pen was another one of the accidents that *could* have happened accidentally. By now, Sam was convinced that someone was purposely trying to hurt Tim.

Tim continued to insist he had no idea who was behind it all. "No, I don't think it was Paul," he said, when Sam broached her growing suspicions to him. "Unless he's a psychic and wrote the letter because he knew I'd fall for you as soon as I saw you." He smiled at her.

Privately, Sam wondered if the letter might just be a coincidence, a genuine crank. Her suspicions hardened after the episode with the bull. The last time she'd seen Paul, he'd been talking to Dave Jeffries. Over near the animal pens.

Paul had always been a little too possessive,

she thought. She still didn't quite believe he'd try to kill someone. He was more likely to start a fight—out in the open. Her lingering doubts, though, had pushed her farther away from him than she'd ever been in her life. And Tim was there to catch her, arms open.

She hadn't forgotten Nicole's warnings, or Helen's thinly veiled hints, or even the implications of the gossip magazine. But she didn't care anymore. When she was with Tim, none of it was important, and the future seemed far away. They talked about his career in movies, her riding, how beautiful the mountains were. The one subject they never mentioned was what would happen after the end of filming, although the time was drawing close.

Thursday afternoon, as Sam was throwing the last bag of trash into the back of the pickup, Nicole called to her. "Sam! Wait a minute!"

Sam turned. She hadn't seen much of Nicole in recent days, because of the increased work load.

"Hi," Nicole said. "This business of working six days a week gets old. Anyway, they won't need me tomorrow or the next day. They're shooting some buddy stuff with Mick and Tim, so I'm off. I haven't been anyplace besides Agua

Verde in *weeks*. No offense—there isn't much to do there. Want to go into Tucson? I'd like to see some more of Arizona. Like the stores." She grinned.

Sam laughed at Nicole's idea of tourist attractions, but agreed. Nicole had already invited Helen. Since neither of them had a car with her, they'd go in Sam's pickup. That evening, Sam arranged with her mother to take an extra turn later in exchange for some time off. The three girls were going shopping.

Friday morning they set out from the Lizardfoot in Sam's old green Dodge. All three were ready for a break. Sam had never worked so hard during a summer vacation in her life. Only when she was free from the food chores and Tim was busy did she have time to practice with Twigs or think about what would happen when the film was over. Tim would go back to California—she knew that. What Sam didn't know was what would come next. They could call and write letters, and possibly visit each other, but Sam still had her senior year ahead of her at Agua Verde High. And deep inside, she wasn't sure Tim would continue a long-distance relationship.

Even though she was past due for some time off, Sam wasn't all that eager to spend the day with the other two girls. In fact, she'd have been happy to spend the day all by herself, far away from the Lizardfoot Ranch and the tension that had recently descended upon it. She'd found a note that morning, an unstamped envelope with her name on the outside. Someone had managed to put the envelope on the nightstand by her bed while she was asleep. It had held a sheet of plain paper with a single typed line: "Get away from Tim Rafferty before you get hurt."

Whoever had left that note had been in Sam's bedroom, and whoever it was might be a killer. Sam immediately thought of Paul; he'd have no trouble getting around the Phillipses' house in the dark. But then she remembered the similar threat Tim had received. There was no way that Paul could have sent Tim that letter.

It didn't really matter who had sent the warning, it had been effective. Sam was scared. She was already worried about Tim, but now it looked like whoever was after Tim was after her, too.

Sam almost canceled the shopping trip. Realistically, anyone could have left the note on the table, and both Nicole and Helen had tried to warn her off Tim.

As they piled into the pickup, Nicole asked, "How old is this thing anyway?"

Sam grinned as she started the engine. "It's a '71."

"That's older than I am!" Nicole's appalled reaction made both Sam and Helen crack up.

"It was the main ranch truck for years; then my older brother got it when he turned sixteen. He got a car when he graduated from college last year, and I got the Green Beast."

Helen added, "Before we moved to Beverly Hills, my mom's car was over twenty years old. She's got a new one now. It's just ten years old."

Nicole made a face. "Okay, go ahead and laugh. But I'm used to newer ones."

It was the first time Sam had stopped to consider how different their backgrounds were. Nicole's family was wealthy, and she had started in show business at a young age. The contrast with Sam's own life was dramatic. She tried to fit Helen into the picture. "You live in Beverly Hills, Helen?" Sam asked. "Where were you before that?"

"St. Johns, Montana. We just moved a couple

years ago," Helen said. "A little town a lot like Agua Verde. I miss it."

It was the most she'd said about herself so far. "How'd you get started working in movies?" Sam asked.

Helen shrugged. "I used to ride in competitions, back in St. Johns. About a year ago, someone Mom knew called her because they were doing a commercial and needed someone who could ride."

"Ah ha!" Nicole crowed. "I knew I'd seen you someplace. That was the Blacksnake Boots ad, wasn't it?"

As they went on, Helen's shyness finally started to melt, along with some of Sam's suspicions. Sam found herself describing life on the ranch as it normally was, and telling Nicole what the movie had wrong. Helen admitted her shyness was a problem. She told Sam and Nicole she really didn't want a career in movies anyway; she was saving the money she was earning for college and planned to become a vet. Nicole dreamed aloud about the parts she wanted to play someday. She was serious about her career, and she wanted solid roles.

When they arrived in Tucson, they parked at

a mall and got out. Sam started to head for the stores.

"Aren't you going to lock the truck?" Nicole asked.

"Green Beast is theft-proof," Sam said with a grin. "Half the time I even forget to take the keys out. Who's going to steal a beat-up truck that's this old? And besides, you have to know how to handle it. I'll bet neither one of you can drive it."

"Why not?" Nicole asked. "It's old, but I can handle a stick shift."

"It doesn't look too different from Mom's car," Helen added.

"Bet me." Sam grinned. "When we come out, I'll let both of you try it. You'll get stuck."

They went on into the mall and Nicole proceeded to lead them into a small shop that specialized in turquoise jewelry. While Sam had drooled over some of the items in the window before, she'd never gone in, knowing that the prices were much too high for her budget. They didn't slow Nicole down at all.

"I'm still underage, so most of what I make goes into a trust fund, but I get a pretty generous allowance," she said. "And there's always plastic." The inlaid silver bracelet she got was only the first purchase of the afternoon. They went on to the next store, Sam shaking her head. Even Helen thought the prices were low compared to L.A. As the day wore on, all three of them found items they liked. Sam splurged on a denim skirt and matching vest.

Despite herself, Sam had fun. But always at the back of her mind, clouding her enjoyment, was the memory of that note. Either one of them could have left it, and Sam couldn't think of anyone else who would have.

Tim was up on Lee's Flat, where the tedious process of moviemaking dragged on. During one break, he and Mick went back to get sodas. Even at the higher elevation of the plateau, the day was hot, and the air was no longer dry. With the approach of the summer monsoons, the humidity was building daily. The tub that earlier in the day contained ice and sodas held mainly water, but the cans were still cool and the contents wet. They each got one and headed back to the filming.

Mick took a long swig, then said, "Tim, what do you plan to do once we finish here?"

Tim knew what Mick was talking about. The other actor had been playing older brother to

Sam since they'd been on location. But he didn't want to talk about her with Mick. "Take some time off, first thing. My agent says he has a couple of guest star roles he wants me to look at, and he's still talking to the producers on that science fiction deal."

"I mean about Sam." This time, Mick wouldn't be put off. "She's a nice kid. I don't want her hurt."

"She's more than nice—she's terrific. And I'm not going to hurt her, dammit!"

"Tim, you've got a bad rep with girlfriends," Mick said.

"I've had a lot of girls, yeah." Tim had heard this lecture too many times from his guardian. "That doesn't mean I'm using them and it doesn't mean I'm hurting them. If nobody had ever heard of me and I was just some guy in high school, do you think the tabloids and everybody would be on my case this way? Those dudes can change girlfriends without it being a big deal."

"All right, I'll give you that," Mick said. "But maybe girls fall just a little harder because of who you are. Think about it. And even if you *were* just some high school jerk, I'd tell you the same thing. Don't hurt Sammie."

Tim didn't want to listen to any more. He'd never tried to hurt anyone—in fact, he'd tried hard not to. Mick had known him for years, and he'd never come on like this before. Of course, he'd never been friends with Tim's girlfriend before, either.

Tim wondered how Sam was getting along with Nicole and Helen in Tucson. Especially with Helen. Could Helen be the one trying to set him up? It was hard to believe; she seemed like such a nice girl. Sure, things hadn't worked out between him and the stunt rider, but that was ancient history. Besides, Tim had traced her movements. It was impossible to tie Helen to the accidents.

When Helen had first shown up at the ranch, Tim had suspected that she was the one who'd sent him that threat letter. Then he'd checked out her handwriting on the stunt script where she was making notes. Helen's neat script was nothing like the writing in the note. But Helen could have faked the handwriting in the note, and she could have set up the accidents so that she always had a strong alibi when they happened. Tim couldn't think of anyone else associated with *West Wind* who had a reason to hurt him. It had to be Helen. He just hoped he could prove it before it was too late.

It was late afternoon by the time the trio emerged from the giant mall. Once they were back in the truck, Sam remembered what they'd talked about earlier. She pulled onto a side street and parked, then had Nicole get behind the wheel.

"It's an H pattern for shifting, right?" Nicole asked. She tried to put the truck into first gear and couldn't. "What's wrong with this thing?"

Sam just grinned and motioned for her to climb out. She slid over, got the truck into first, then told Helen, "Your turn. Start it in first gear." She and Nicole went around and got back into the cab; then Helen started the truck.

She pulled away from the curb with no trouble and smiled in triumph. "Told you I could handle old cars," she said.

"Just wait," Sam promised. As they picked up speed, Helen tried to shift into second gear. The gearshift jammed, and the engine raced in neutral when she stepped on the gas. They drifted to a stop as she tried to get the stubborn lever to move. The truck died again with a shudder.

"Told you it was theft-proof," Sam said, re-claiming her place behind the wheel. "It's not worth fixing, not for what it would cost. Anyway, if you don't know how to shift just right it hangs up between gears." She jiggled the lever and managed to free it once more, then demonstrated to the others how it was done. "I get sloppy sometimes, and then it happens to me. One of these days it'll break, and we'll have to junk it."

Nicole was incredulous. "And you mean to say you drive this thing around and never know if it's going to break down and strand you?" She waved her hand toward the Catalina Mountains, rugged and spectacular in the sunset light. "What if you were up there someplace?"

"I'd have to hike out," Sam said. "That's why I always tell somebody where I'm going. Or almost always," she added, thinking of her ill-fated ride with Tim in his Bronco.

Sam wished she'd had a chance earlier in the summer to get to know Nicole and Helen this way. Her suspicions about the note were forgotten. She didn't even mind when Nicole teased her about Tim again.

"How about you and Dave?" she tossed back.

"I'm almost ready to give up on him," Nicole

said. "I like to have fun dating a guy, and he's not there half the time. Then, when he does pay attention, he's too gloomy. I don't know what that guy's problem is, but he needs to lighten up."

"Stunt riding is dangerous," Helen said seriously. "He's always checking the gear and making sure it's safe. I think Dave wants to be a stunt coordinator someday."

"Ever seen Rick Moore off the set?" Nicole was referring to *West Wind*'s stunt coordinator. "Sure, on the job he's careful—that's how young stunt men get to be old stunt men. But he doesn't worry once he's off the set."

"Like Tim," Sam added. "He's not acting when the cameras aren't rolling."

"Don't bet on that." Helen's voice was level. "He's done it for so long, he doesn't even know when he's acting anymore."

"What do you mean?" Sam asked.

There was a long pause, so long Sam began to wonder if Helen would speak again before they got to the ranch. "You think Tim's in love with you, don't you?" Helen finally asked. "That's what I meant. He's acting a part again, and he probably doesn't even know it himself."

Sam's earlier misgivings about Helen came

back with a rush. "You know, I'm getting tired of everyone warning me about Tim," she said. "Just because he's an actor, nobody thinks he can really care about me."

"That's not so," Helen interrupted. "It's not because he's an actor. It's because he's Tim Rafferty."

Sam looked over at Helen, seated in the center, then turned her eyes back to the road. "That's a pretty nasty crack." All of a sudden, the day was ruined.

"I'm sorry," Helen spoke quietly. "I'm not trying to make nasty cracks. I enjoyed myself today, and I'm tired of playing games and hiding. I knew Tim before the show started. I knew him before I left St. Johns."

The truck swerved as Sam's grip on the wheel tightened. Keeping her eyes on the road, she said, "What's that got to do with what you said? And why haven't you said anything before now?" On the other side of Helen, Nicole was silent.

Helen took a deep breath. "I think you can guess. Tim was on location in St. Johns. I fell in love with him almost as soon as I met him. And he fell for me as well. That's the thing with Tim —he's been acting for so long he believes himself. He always means it when he falls in love. He just doesn't stay that way."

"After he stopped writing letters, Mom got a job offer from some friends in L.A.," she went on. "When we got to L.A., I called Tim. It was like he'd never heard of me. I think it was the first time that had happened, having a girl he'd dropped call him. He was embarrassed."

"Why did you take the part in *West Wind*? Are you still chasing him?" As she said it, Sam realized it was unfair; Helen hadn't been chasing Tim. But Sam was angry.

"No." Even in the darkened cab, Sam could see Helen shaking her head. "Like I told you, they called me. I knew Dave from some extra work I did with him, and he asked Rick to hire me. I don't think Dave knew about Tim and me. When I heard Tim was starring, I wanted to say no, but it was too good a job to pass up. I talked it over with Dave; then I called Tim and told him I was going to be here and asked him to leave me alone. I think he would have anyway."

"I thought that was it," Nicole said softly. "I could tell something was bothering Tim, and he almost never says anything to you. And you've been so shy it didn't seem real. Stunt doubles may not have any lines, but that camera is on you. Someone that shy wouldn't be able to handle it."

"Anyway, that's the story," Helen concluded. "You've been nice to me, Sam, and I don't want to see you get hurt. I think you should drop Tim before you do. You still have Paul; he's a cute guy. Otherwise, you *will* get hurt."

Sam didn't answer. She wanted to ask Tim about that letter again. Maybe it really had been anonymous, and maybe it had been from Helen. But even if Helen had written the letter, she might not be the one behind the accidents. It might explain Tim's reluctance to tell Sheriff McBride about it, though.

She was sure Helen had left her the note that morning. Helen kept talking about Tim hurting people, just like the letter and the note. Sam found it hard to believe that Helen could have caused all the accidents by herself. She hadn't ruled out Paul. The letters could be coincidence, or collusion. Twice Sam had almost been hurt in accidents meant for Tim, the broken curb chain and the brakes on the Bronco.

Either way, Helen still resented Tim. As for her warnings—he might have dropped girlfriends in the past, but that didn't mean he'd drop Sam. If the letters were just jealousy, she could ignore them. But she had to talk to Tim soon.

All conversation in the truck had died. Sam reached down to flip on the radio. They were in the mountains now and the Tucson station kept fading in and out. The Green Beast didn't have a tape player, so it was the radio or nothing. She fiddled with the dial, trying to get decent reception on any station, even ones she usually ignored. She finally gave up. The silence stretched out unbroken.

After a quarter of an hour had passed, Helen said, "Sam, I'm sorry. Why do you think I haven't said anything up till now? I knew you'd be upset. I just couldn't watch you go through the same thing I did without saying something."

"Sammie," Nicole added. "I told you Tim and I dated for a while. He's a sweet guy, really. I don't think he means to hurt anyone. A while back some gossip columnist said Tim was the kiss of death for anyone he fell in love with. It was all supposed to be based on some girl who died because of him. Anyway, don't blame Helen for the stories."

"And the letters?" Sam asked sharply.

"What letters?" Nicole sounded puzzled. Helen said nothing.

"I found a note this morning," Sam said, her eyes fixed on the road before them. "Warning me to stay away from Tim."

"I didn't write it," Helen said, her voice quiet. "A lot of people know about Tim. It sounds like good advice, but don't blame me for it."

"I'm not blaming anyone," Sam said. She hoped they couldn't tell the effort it took to keep her voice level. "I'm going to talk to Tim. You're wrong about him. And anyway, I don't care. I love him." *Love.* She'd carefully avoided the word before, even in her thoughts. It was such a final word. But she'd said it now. She was in love with Tim Rafferty.

As they came within sight of Lizard Peak, Sam caught a glimpse of glaring white lights on the side of the mountain. For a moment, she wondered what they were. Then she realized; those were the lights for the movie. Nicole spoke for the first time in half an hour. "They're running a little late, I see. They were supposed to finish for the day at ten." Her voice was normal, as though the earlier conversation hadn't taken place at all.

Sam tried to see her watch, then gave up.

"What time is it?" The old Dodge didn't have a clock.

"It's ten thirty," Helen answered, her voice hesitant.

"I'm glad I don't have to come down that road in the dark," Nicole said. "Thank God they don't have me in any night scenes up there! Once we finish the mountain stuff, we'll be almost done." Sam felt a pang at the reminder of how close the movie was to completion. Another thing to discuss with Tim.

They drove on; then Helen's diffident voice came again. "What's that red light up there near the set?"

Sam looked up at the mountain again and skidded to a halt. She stared for a moment, making sure of what she saw, then started so abruptly both the others were thrown back against the seat. She put her foot down on the accelerator, glad they were almost to the ranch. As they bounced across the potholes, she swore under her breath.

"Sammie, what is it?" Nicole asked.

Sam kept her foot down. "Fire."

TEN

Sam had the truck door open before she turned off the key. She didn't bother to remove it; she was already sprinting for the ranch house. The lights were still on in the back of the house, and for once she was glad her mother always waited up for her. Behind her, Nicole and Helen hurried in.

Her mother came out of the kitchen, yawning. "Good grief, Sam, it's quarter to eleven. You're a little late."

"Mom, there's a fire up below Lee's Flat," Sam interrupted. "Do they have a radio up at the set?"

Her mother woke up abruptly. She sent Sam after her father and headed to the base radio in the corner. Jack Phillips had insisted they keep one of the ranch's radios on the remote set. His insistence might save lives now.

Within a short time, they had a picture of the situation. It wasn't good. Shooting had just finished. Some of the cars had started down and encountered the brush fire. It straddled the dirt road, making it too dangerous to drive through, so they'd turned back. Dozens of people were trapped—there was no other easy way off the plateau. A steep path led down the cliff. It would be tricky at night even for an experienced climber. As an evacuation route for that many people, it would be too dangerous to risk short of desperation. Even if they could make it down the cliff, tens of thousands of dollars' worth of equipment would be lost if the fire swept over the site.

After radioing the film crew, Marion started calling some of the nearby ranches. Normally, brush fires in the high country were watched and not fought. Jack Phillips sometimes said if he saw a fire, he'd fan the flames, since burning the brush improved the grazing. This one couldn't be ignored. They had some fire-fighting equipment; they'd soon find out whether or not it was enough.

Paul and his father were the first to arrive, since their ranch was the closest. They got there just as Jack finished filling the water truck. Usually he hauled water out to stock ponds, but the pump could put water on a fire as well. Sam had the pump packs out and was filling them with water. Paul joined her, slinging his shovels and heavy gloves in the back of Green Beast. They'd fought one fire together before, when it had threatened the Cradle X headquarters.

By the time they headed up the mountain, less than a half hour after Helen had spotted the fire, it was an organized effort. Sylvie and Jack were in the water truck, which they'd drive as close to the blaze as possible. Sam and Paul bounced along behind the water truck in Sam's pickup. Others would follow with their own hand tools.

Marion was coordinating things from the ranch radio. Sam had grabbed one of the portable units, and her dad had one in the water truck so they could stay in touch. Communications were crucial during a fire. Marion radioed the people trapped above the flames to make firebreaks around the area. It was a good suggestion, but there wasn't any equipment for it on the set.

To Sam's surprise, Helen had joined them in Green Beast. Sam wasn't sure if the stunt rider had any business being there, but every pair of hands would be needed. Sam kept her suspicions to herself. Helen couldn't have had anything to do with the fire, even if she had caused the other accidents. Sam had been with her and Nicole. As for Paul, Sam knew he'd never start a fire when the fire danger was this high. Wildfires could burn out of control, sweeping thousands of acres and ranches. He wouldn't risk it, even if he was behind the accidents.

When they got near the fire, Sam parked the truck and they scrambled out. Paul helped Helen put on a pump pack and explained how it worked, while Sam strapped one on herself. It was heavy, but it would become lighter all too soon as the water in the unit was exhausted. They headed toward the edge of the fire nearest the road. They had to put out the fire along the road first.

Helen pumped the handle of her pack and watched the heavy spray shoot out to a surprising distance.

"Pace yourself. Your arms'll get tired awfully

fast doing this. I'll lead on this side. Sam, you want to flank me?"

She got to within twenty feet of the blaze, the wand in her left hand. With her right hand Sam pumped vigorously, sliding the mechanism back and forth rapidly. Water spurted onto the fire. Paul did the same on her left. The tank truck was pumping water on the other side of the road, as Sylvie worked the electric pump and Jack used the hose. "Make the water last," he shouted over the crackle of the flames. "It'll take too long to get back down for more. If we can get through first, we can get everyone out."

They inched forward attacking the fire. It was a slow-moving fire, and there was a good chance they could break through by following the road. The wind had died down, and fires at night usually burned downslope instead of up, as the cool air from the high places flowed down into the valleys. Others arrived and started work behind them, shoveling dirt on the embers to make sure the fire was out.

The heat was intense, and Sam's eyes burned from the fumes. She aimed the pump wand at a tangled mesquite thicket. Dense, choking smoke rolled over her. Behind her Helen was coughing but still trying to keep her own stream pointed at the brush. Sam blinked hard, trying to clear the tears from her eyes, and stepped closer. A charred branch shifted under her foot, and she nearly fell. Struggling to stay upright, she shot a stream of water on the char. Mud underfoot was better than live embers.

Little by little, the group advanced upward, led by the pack pumps on the right and Jack with the hose on the left. Behind the hose and pumps, the workers with hand tools made sure there weren't any hot spots ready to flare back to life behind them. Downed yuccas were particularly dangerous, able to smolder for a long time. Fires sometimes restarted from such hot spots days after they were supposedly out.

Sam's arms ached and her lungs hurt from breathing the acrid smoke. But the fire wasn't very wide, and the other side was in sight. Helen's water ran out and she stumbled back to the rear, just minutes before Paul made it past the fire and into the burned-out region beyond it.

With the road secured, the movie crew was safe. The fire burned unchecked on either side of the road, covering about fifty acres and still moving sideways. Luckily, the breeze earlier in the evening had caused the fire to spread more across the face of the slope than up or down. They had needed only to fight their way across an acre or so of burn. But while the distance by road was under a half a mile, it would have been impossible to drive that half-mile.

A couple of the production crew's electricians in a Jeep were watching on the other side. As soon as the fire crew broke through, they cheered and came to meet them. After a few words with Jack, one of them sped back up to the location to spread the word that the road was clear and to round up some extra fire fighters. The hardest part would be digging more firebreaks. The fire could still turn and sweep the movie location, and the heavy trucks and vans couldn't be driven out right now. A rocky spur protected one side of the site; an additional firebreak below the edge of Lee's Flat would end the threat. Sylvie drove back down the mountain to refill the tank truck, taking Helen with her. When Sylvie got back, she'd stand by in case water was needed again. Meanwhile, there was still work to do.

Tim and John were in the first truck to come down from the set. They stopped at the edge of the burn and got out, leaving the motor running and the lights on. John looked at black ground visible in the headlights. He turned to look at the glow to the left, where flames were still visible as the blaze claimed more mesquites, then came over to the weary cluster of fire fighters. Tim slowly followed.

The crescent moon had risen by now, but it didn't give much light. It was bright enough, however, to show the smudges and grime and soot on the faces of the fire fighters. The tear tracks from reddened eyes and the exhaustion were visible in the slumped figures.

Tim came over to where Sam and Paul were standing. Ignoring both Paul's presence and her sweaty, filthy condition, he pulled her into a close embrace. Sam was too aware of Paul's eyes on them to respond to Tim's kiss. She pulled away after a moment.

Tim's eyes met Paul's. "Thanks for helping to get us out."

"You weren't in any danger," Paul said. His tone was rude. Sam figured he didn't want Tim's gratitude.

"They weren't in as much danger as they could have been," she corrected. "Any fire is dangerous, especially with the brush as dry as it is this time of the year. If we hadn't cleared the road, they might still have been okay by morning, but if the fire had turned, or the wind had come up—"

"They could have gone down the trail on the far side, over the cliff." Then Paul added, grudgingly, " 'Course, it might have been rough at night, especially for anybody afraid of heights."

"I've seen the trail," Tim said. "It would have been hell trying to get everyone down, especially with just the moon for light. I don't think we could have made it, not without an accident." He paused on the last word; at least this time there'd been no accidents. Then he asked Sam, "Now what happens with the fire?"

"We get back to work," Paul answered. Behind Tim, Jack was motioning them over. "We need to make another firebreak."

When they joined Mr. Phillips, he suggested that Sam and Paul go down with the movie crew. "You kids were in the front line and you did a good job. We're not trying to put out the whole fire, just make sure it stays below the plateau. Pat's crew just got here, so they can handle the shovels. You've done your share."

The suggestion made Sam aware of how worn out she was. All her muscles ached, and she desperately wanted a shower to get the smoke out of her eyes and hair. "Thanks, Dad. I think we will." She gave her father a quick peck on a cheek that tasted of smoke, then turned to go. She swayed slightly as she let herself feel the weariness. The truck was almost three-quarters of a mile away.

Paul steadied her with a hand on her arm, then said, "Want me to go get the truck?"

She yawned, startling herself, and shook her head. "No, I'll be fine. I'll let you drive, though —my eyes won't stop watering." More truthfully, her eyes didn't want to stay open any longer. She took a couple of steps, then realized Tim was still standing there. "You want to ride down with us, Tim?"

She hoped he'd say yes. Despite the way they'd worked together on the fire, she didn't want to be alone with Paul. She had too many questions, and she was too tired to ask them. One eye on Paul, Tim agreed. Paul said nothing, and the three picked their way down the steep slope to the truck.

"After they clear a break, what'll they do?" Tim asked.

Sam shrugged. "The fire will burn itself out. Dad'll keep an eye on it—he always does. Even when we just let a fire go, we watch it. You should be able to get back up here by tomorrow, or at least by the next day."

"That's good," Tim said. "We're behind schedule."

It was the first reminder Sam'd had in hours that the end of filming and Tim's departure were both near. But at that moment she was too exhausted to think of anything except a shower and sleep.

By morning the fire had died on its own. The burn covered about 120 acres, which made it a medium-sized brush fire. The black scar on the side of Lizard Peak was easily visible, but it would be covered by new grass as soon as the monsoons started. Natural fires were healthy for rangeland, clearing dead grass and brush.

Filming started late the day after the fire, but as John told the Phillipses, "I'm just glad we're able to shoot at all." He had stopped by the house before heading up to the location and spent some time with Jack going over the extent and cost of the fire. The film company would pay the costs of fighting the fire, since it would have been left unchecked had they not been there. There wasn't much expense involved, mainly the cost of extra water and pumping. A couple of fire fighters had gotten minor burns. The worst injury hadn't involved any of the fire fighters at all. Mick had stopped to talk to the fire crew shortly after Sam had left. Moonlight and rough ground were a bad combination; he'd tripped and landed on his hands and knees. It would have been a minor incident, but he had landed on a chunk of still-smoldering yucca. His right hand was badly burned.

At one point, the fire had burned right to the edge of the firebreak. Without the break, the production could have lost much of the equipment on the mountain. Even though it was insured, the loss would have been a major blow to the film company. As it was, since the fire had been kept below the rim of the plateau, they wouldn't even have to reshoot any footage; the burned area wasn't visible.

Later that day, Jack and Sam went up in the ultralight to check for hot spots. One person could have managed easily enough—Sam went along because she enjoyed a chance to ride with her dad in the two-seater. They flew low over the set, giving her a chance to wave at Tim. Even from a couple of hundred feet up, she could see him grinning at her as he waved back.

That evening, when she drove up with the food for the supper break, Tim came into the chuck wagon. "That looked like fun," he said as he grabbed a handful of tortilla chips. "But I still can't get used to the idea of a rancher using a plane instead of a horse or a Jeep."

"Dad was in the Air Force in Vietnam," Sam said. "He's flown most of his life. Ultralights are efficient, but a lot of ranchers just don't think of flying as an answer. Of course, most of them have more flat land than we do. Half our range-land's too rough for trucks. You ride in, or you hike, or you fly over it. And an ultralight lets you stay close enough to the ground to see things."

"And besides, he loves it," Tim finished with a grin. He was standing beside her as she laid out the trays of food, and reached past her for another handful of chips. "Don't kid me. It may be efficient, but it's fun as well."

"I've never denied it." Sam grinned, too.

"Think you can take me up?" he asked. "I've never flown in an ultralight."

"I'll ask Dad, but don't tell too many people, or we'll have half the cast wanting to go up! And don't tell John."

"Yeah, he'd tell me to let Dave go instead,"

Tim said. "I can't blame him, but I get tired of the mother hen bit. By the way, what's with him and your aunt? That looks pretty serious."

"It is," Sam said. "They don't want to announce it yet, but they're getting married after the filming's done." Aunt Sylvie had told her just that morning. Sam wasn't surprised; they were natural together.

"John has good taste," Tim said. He slipped an arm around her waist and with his free hand turned her face toward him. "Of course, so do I." He cupped her chin with his hand and leaned forward for a kiss.

Much later, after the meal and the cleanup and the trip back down the mountain in the dark, Sam was still thinking of that kiss. Aunt Sylvie would be moving to Los Angeles soon with John. She was free to go wherever she wanted and do as she chose, and so was John. Sam still had a year of school. And even if she were as free as Aunt Sylvie, she didn't know what Tim wanted. Or what she wanted herself.

ELEVEN

Sam's father reluctantly gave her permission to take Tim up in the ultralight. She waited for Tim to come down the mountain that night from filming, but it finally got to be too late. Leaving a note on the door of Tim's trailer, she went to bed. She'd take him flying the next day.

Tim was ready in the morning. There was a scheduled break in filming, so Tim had the day off. It was a perfect day for flying, warming up fast, with light breezes but no strong gusts. Sam took him out to the barn, where they walked the two-seater out. Seeing the craft up close for the first time, he was a little leery of its apparently flimsy construction.

"Hey, these are probably the safest aircraft

ever built!" Sam said. "You don't even need a pilot's license to fly one."

"Really?" Tim didn't look convinced.

"You'll see," she promised. She pointed out the various safety features, all as simple as the plane itself. When he asked about parachutes, wondering if they needed them, she shook her head.

"I'm not sure you *could* parachute from one of these things, and I don't think it would be safe to try it," she said. "There is a parachute for the whole aircraft. See that thing there?" She pointed to something slung under the seats that looked like a fat rocket. "That's the ballistic parachute. If I have to use it, it shoots out— that's why it's called ballistic—to the side there, so it misses the props, and it's tethered here. The whole chute slides up that cable to the top, and you float down on that."

He looked at it again. "Impressive. Also a little scary. Ever have to use it?"

She shook her head. "Uh uh. Really, it's for emergencies only, and I mean bad ones. Like the plane coming apart in midair or something. That's not going to happen. These things are *safe*, Tim. Otherwise my dad wouldn't let me go up by myself."

"All right, I'll take your word for it." He grinned at her. "Now are we going to go flying or not?"

They strapped themselves into the seats, which were mounted side by side instead of behind each other, and soon they were in the air. Despite the deafening noise from the engine, there was a lazy, peaceful feel about it. They were low enough and going slowly enough that things on the ground were easily visible. It was the closest thing to being a bird Sam could imagine. She thought back to the Harris hawk she and Tim had watched from the ridge a few weeks before. If she saw it, she'd try to circle it, like a larger hawk.

They climbed over Lee's Flat, and she pointed out the burn to Tim. He had relaxed and was enjoying himself now. She circled for another look when the engine suddenly coughed and died.

In the unexpected silence, Tim said, "Safe, huh?" He kept his voice light, but she could see the white knuckles as he grasped the side of his seat.

"I've had engines quit on me before," she said. "Probably just a clogged fuel line." She banked gently toward the peak and then felt the quiver that meant she'd caught a thermal. She let out a breath she hadn't known she was holding.

"Safe, when you've had engines quit?" Tim still sounded upset, but he relaxed his grip slightly. His knuckles were no longer bloodless.

"They're designed like hang gliders," she said. "As a matter of fact, that's basically what they are. All losing the engine means is that we're limited to riding the air currents and thermals. Which we're doing right now, by the way. Does it look like we're crashing?"

The question was rhetorical—they were gaining altitude. The rising air current up the slopes below Lee's Flat was carrying them higher. The air was being heated by the ground below, baked in an Arizona summer sun. The result was a strong updraft that they could ride for hours, working from one thermal to the next. Sam aimed the light craft back toward the ranch. There was no sense landing several miles away and having to walk home.

Without the loud buzz saw noise of the engine, talking was easier. Tim relaxed again and was enjoying his hawk's-eye view of the world. Sam pointed out some cattle as they passed, showing him how practical the lightweight aircraft were for ranching in rugged country. No one could really understand the difference it made until they were up there and *saw* how much could be seen from the sky.

There was no indication of any unusual trouble, so Sam brought them in close to the ranch and reduced their altitude. The air currents were less dependable here, and there were eddies that could make for a rough landing. She hoped she could set them down in the pasture where Twigs was grazing placidly. She banked toward it; the response felt funny.

As she tried to glide in for a landing, she knew she had real trouble. The flaps weren't working! She glanced toward them as they overshot the pasture. Grimly, she forced the plane into a banking turn and came around for another pass. The pasture wasn't a runway, but it had the advantage of being free of mesquite thickets. Putting down there would be safest.

Tim picked up on her worry. "What's up?" He sat very still, which was the biggest help he could be. "More problems?"

"Flaps are jammed," Sam answered. The ultralight still had tail flaps, but the main flaps on the wings were frozen. "Those movable parts on the back edge of the wing—see 'em? I need to get them up so I can land this thing, and they aren't coming up." She worked the controls again. "Nope, nothing."

"Can you land us?" he asked quietly.

"I'm going to get us as low as I can and then try to stall." As she spoke, she circled the pasture again. She wanted to get as low to the ground as she could before she tried the tricky maneuver. "If we're lucky and I do it right, we'll drop straight down instead of plowing into the ground nose first. This thing doesn't have a nose anyway. We're right out front."

She'd heard her father's description of a stall many times, but she'd never done it before. Tim kept quiet, letting her concentrate on her flying. Their roles were reversed from the accident in the Bronco. Then there had been nothing she could do. Now Tim was helpless. He kept his eyes open as they swung around, ever lower.

Finally, she was as low as she dared go. An ultralight could land as lightly as a cottonwood leaf in the autumn, but it could also crash, killing its passengers. She pushed such thoughts out of her mind and reminded herself how safe ultralights were. It wasn't as if she were trying to bring a 747 in for a dead-stick landing. She concentrated on the mechanics of the landing, then brought them around into the wind. "Cross your fingers and don't move," she warned Tim, then headed over the pasture one last time.

She waited, then suddenly put on full tail flaps, forcing the tail down. Their forward motion halted, and they settled toward the ground. They were almost down when a strong gust of wind caught them and flipped them. For an instant, there was a kaleidoscope of ground and sky and distant cottonwoods, then a jolt as they crashed.

They hung for a moment almost sideways, the craft balanced on its left side and wing. Then with a crunching sound the ultralight shifted, righting itself and coming down on the partially collapsed landing gear. Sam fumbled for the buckle of the safety harness.

Tim undid his own and slid out of the wreckage. "I think both of us had better work on landings," he said shakily. "You messed this thing up about like I did the Bronco."

She stood up, welcoming the solid, stationary earth under her feet. "Dad always says that any landing you can walk away from is a good one. This was a good one." Then Tim caught her as her knees gave way and she started to shake.

The ultralight looked like an aluminum butterfly with crumpled wings. But they were down.

"We were real lucky this time, Tim," Sam said. "What's going on?"

"I wish I knew. All these accidents . . ."

"Accidents!" Sam cut him off. "Someone's trying to kill us, Tim. I want to know who, and I want to know why."

Tim looked at Sam and then at the ground. He shook his head and said, "I don't know."

Sam backed away from him. She didn't know what was going on, and she didn't know who she could trust anymore. "Well, you'd better find out," she ordered. "Because I don't intend to die. And I don't want you to, either."

The next day, filming started early. They were scheduled to do the cliff scenes, and John announced he intended to finish them in one day. Twelve-hour days were common in filmmaking. This one looked as though it might go even longer.

The cliffs were near the path that led down from the plateau, the one they hadn't been forced to use on the night of the fire. Anyone on the cliffs had to wear safety gear. In view of the accidents that had plagued the set, that was probably a good idea.

Tim was sure the accidents were aimed only at him, but he had no way of proving it. As Sam had suspected, the fuel line was clogged on the ultralight. She'd found the explanation for the problem with the flaps almost at once. They were attached to the wing with a simple hinge. The small metal ring that fit through the end of the pin holding this in place was missing. Without the ring, the pin had gradually worked itself almost out, freezing the flaps in position. It could have happened from metal fatigue or a dozen other ways. But she had left a note on the door of Tim's trailer, asking him to go flying. Anyone could have read it.

The garage had called Tim yesterday about the Bronco. They had found the bleed valve open on the brakes, but there was no way of proving it had been done deliberately. A sloppy mechanic could have been responsible. The curb chain could have broken on its own; that happened often enough. The latch on the bull's chute had been jammed, and latches jam on their own sometimes. There wasn't one accident that Tim could *prove* wasn't accidental.

Tim was scared for himself, and he was even

more scared for Sam. Whoever was after him had to have known Sam would pilot the ultralight. That meant the killer no longer cared if anyone else was hurt, as long as Tim died. Tim agreed with Sam, he didn't want to die. And he certainly didn't want Sam to, or anyone else. Was Walt's death his fault? He didn't want to admit that, but sometimes he thought so. Maybe if he'd told Ryder about the letter back when the accidents first started, it could have been stopped.

Whoever it was. That was what bothered him the most. He wondered if Nicole could have written the letter. She'd been pretty nasty about it when they'd broken up, even if they had worked together well on *West Wind*. Tim was still suspicious of Helen. The more he thought about it, the more likely it became that she could have faked the handwriting. If she was smart enough to sabotage a car and an ultralight, she was smart enough to forge a note.

There wasn't even any proof the letter was connected to the accidents. There was that word again: *proof*. After the accident in the Bronco, the sheriff had questioned him a couple times. It had all been very casual, and Tim had the feeling McBride thought it was all publicity stunts. As if Tim would risk his neck—and Sam's—that way!

Considering the obvious dangers of the cliff scenes, he was glad John insisted on having Dave double him. Rock-climbing looked like fun, but Tim wasn't about to try it for real while someone was going around arranging accidents.

According to the script, a tourist had gotten himself stuck on a ledge while Jeb and Lenny were out rock-climbing. The tourist was the stunt coordinator, Rick Moore, who had a lot of rock-climbing experience. Tim and Mick would be shot in close-up on a ledge fifteen feet down from the top. Actual climbing would use Dave and Rick, with the camera pulled way back. A platform for the camera had been set up on another ledge. Like so many things in movies, an incredible amount of effort was going into a section of the story that would last less than twenty minutes on the screen.

Mick called out, "Hey, Tim, c'mere a minute." He had his shirt off, draped over the boulder he was sitting on.

Mick was struggling with the climbing gear he needed for the scene. Since the characters were supposed to be free-climbing, Rick had specified harnesses that would be concealed by their costumes. He wouldn't let them work without the harnesses, even on the ledge. With careful editing and camera angles, it would look as though the actors were actually climbing without ropes.

"I can't get this thing let out," Mick said, pulling at a strap. He swore and let go. "And these blisters don't help any. Give me a hand, will you?"

Tim tried to adjust the strap, but it was stuck. "I think it's jammed, Mick. Better ask Rick to get you a different one."

"Hell, no," Mick said. He tugged at it one last time, then gave up. "I ask him to fix it, and there goes half a day's shooting. This picture's behind schedule anyway. The thing works fine. It's just too tight." He made sure the rope ran freely and checked when it was supposed to. "Yep, no problem on the rope—it's just the fit. Look, swap with me. You're a little smaller—it won't be that tight on you."

They were supposed to call the stunt coordinator in for any equipment trouble, but Mick was right. There wasn't anything wrong with the actual harness, just the size adjustments. And he was also right about losing any more time. Tim was aware of how much money each delay cost the production company, and this time that meant him as well, since he had invested in *West Wind*. He unbuttoned his shirt and exchanged harnesses with Mick. The same strap worked perfectly on Tim's old harness, and Mick was able to adjust it to himself with no trouble. They finished getting ready and went over to watch Rick's part being filmed.

After the solo shots were completed, they made their way down the steep path to the ledge. The main shots were taken to establish the scene. Again and again, Jeb and Lenny argued about how to rescue the stranded tourist. Again and again, the tourist slipped farther. Again and again, the two stopped arguing and swung down over the edge of the cliff. Rick huddled on another ledge, far below.

This was the only part of the scene that really needed the safety gear. They were supposed to let themselves down over the edge, appearing to be climbing down to the stranded tourist. After editing, it would look as though they were on the sheer cliff, climbing from a point halfway down the face. After four takes, Mick called for a halt.

"I'm not having any luck today with these blasted rigs," he muttered to Tim. "The rope's hanging up." He tugged on the thin line again, then said, "Ready." He knelt beside Tim, peering over the edge, in position for the shot.

"Very quiet, please," the second AD called, and scattered people echoed, *"Quiet!"*

"Roll, please. . . . Rolling! Marker. . . . *Action!"*

Instantly back into character, Tim said, "We can't wait any longer! He's liable to fall at any second!" From below, Rick's voice called, "Help me . . . please!" The grips moved the shiny boards as Mick said, "Idiot tourist. You're right, Jeb, we've got to get him *now*. Follow me." He twisted around and slithered over the edge on his belly.

As Tim followed, John yelled, *"Cut!"* This was the point at which the action was supposed to stop, the point where they'd stopped four times already. Tim was hauling himself back up when Mick said, "No . . ."

Before Tim could do or say anything, Mick fell, sliding down the rock.

Mick slipped twenty feet then stopped, his feet finding a precarious perch on a small outcrop. Tim twisted in his harness, trying to see below him. Above, on top of the cliff, there were shouts as people scrambled for ropes. Tim hauled himself up and knelt down, looking over the edge. He didn't realize it was the same pose as the opening shot.

Mick hugged the rock, trying to hold on to the sheer surface and keep his footing. The blisters on his burnt hand were being scraped raw by the rough rock. Without looking up, he called to Tim, "This wasn't in the script."

"Mick!" Tim's voice was harsh with fear. "Hang on!"

"I'm trying," Mick said. There was a tremor as he added, "I don't know how long I can."

There was a shout from the top of the cliff, and Dave Jeffries yelled, "I'm coming!" He came down the path too fast for safety, carrying a rope, and swung out onto the ledge. Dropping to his knees beside Tim, he called out, "Mick! I'm letting down a rope. There's a loop in the end. If you can get it over you, we can pull you up." His face pale, he shoved the rope at Tim and snapped, "You'll have to help." Carefully, he started letting the rope down. Tim held on to the slack, ready to pull as soon as Mick had the other end. He leaned out to watch, holding his breath.

The loop reached Mick, only inches to one side. Dave told him, "All right, Mick. Let go with one hand and get the rope." Mick edged one hand over and captured the loop, then pulled it back to him. "Now," Dave said, "get it over your head."

Mick leaned out slightly, trying to pull the rope over his head. He let go of the rope for a moment, as the rough texture bit into his raw flesh. The rope swung slightly away from his hand and as it did, his foot slipped on the outcrop. He grabbed at the rope with both hands but missed, knocking it farther away.

With a scream, Mick fell the rest of the way to the base of the cliff, 200 feet below.

Dave continued to kneel on the ledge, his face fixed in horror. Rick rappelled down the cliff as fast as he could. Mick was dead, crumpled like an old rag doll a child had tossed aside. John radioed for help, but there was no real help possible at this point. All anyone could do now was recover the body.

Sam was waiting for Tim when he got back to the ranch. Her mother had taken the radio call from John. She'd told Sam and Sylvie before she called Sheriff McBride. Sam had made an additional call as soon as her mom had finished the official one. It was horrible, but Jackie had to be told. Sam was deeply grateful when Mrs. McBride answered instead of Jackie. It might be cowardly—still, she couldn't face telling Jackie herself. She broke the news to Mrs. McBride, knowing she'd relay it to Jackie as gently as possible.

When Tim walked in with John, Sam ran right into his arms, clinging to him. She'd held back her sobs until then, almost too numb to feel anything. Seeing Tim was a release. As though her presence was a release for him, too, Tim started to cry as well.

"It's too much, Sam," he said. He held her tightly, her face buried in his chest. "Two people dead," he said grimly. "Who is *doing* this?"

Sam tipped her head back and looked at his face. She could feel a tremor go through his arms. The adults had gone into the other room; they were alone. "Tim? You think it wasn't an accident?"

"I *know* it wasn't, dammit!" He swallowed hard and added, "It should have been me. Every single accident that's happened, I should have been the one hurt!"

"Tim, maybe this really was—" Sam began.

"Mick couldn't get his safety rig adjusted, so

we swapped," he cut her off. "He was wearing my harness."

Sam closed her eyes, unable to look at the pain on his face any longer. "You'll have to tell the sheriff," she said quietly.

"I know," he said. "And it's not going to be easy. I should have told him weeks ago."

The remainder of that day and the next were a confused nightmare for everyone who had anything to do with the Lizardfoot Ranch or *West Wind*. There was general disbelief at first. John lost his temper. The sheriff threatened to close down the production, first calling Tim a ghoul for trying to gain publicity, then suggesting Tim had set up the accidents himself. The state police were called, as were the film company lawyers.

Later, Sam couldn't begin to remember all that was said and done during those horrible hours. Except for one phone call. It stood clear in her memory. John called Mick's family and told them there had been an accident. As she listened, Tim's arm around her, she realized just how impossible it was to break such news gently.

* * *

Mick's body was flown back to California, where his family lived. The police went over every incident since Tim had arrived at the Lizardfoot. The harness Mick had started with, ironically, was safe. The jammed strap that had led Mick to trade gear with Tim was a true accident. The harness Tim had given to Mick, on the other hand, showed clear signs of tampering.

The sheriff had a personal interest in the case now. Not only had he liked Mick, but he had to face his daughter. Jackie was shattered. Sam went to see her one time, and felt helpless as Jackie sobbed in her arms. Her feuds with Jackie evaporated in shared grief. Sam didn't even try to answer Jackie's incoherent accusation that it should have been Tim. There was no answer.

Reluctantly, Tim told the authorities about his earlier ties to Helen. She was questioned for hours. Sam described the note she'd found, but it had vanished. The threatening letter Tim had gotten was long since destroyed. Helen denied having written either, and there wasn't a shred of evidence against her. Nicole was questioned as well; it was no secret she had also dated Tim.

The sheriff wasn't limiting his investigation

to Tim's former girlfriends. He'd quizzed Sam. It was obvious he thought it was all a publicity stunt gone hellishly wrong. Tim was the prime suspect for that, but Sheriff McBride also asked Sam questions about John, Larry Cabot, the second AD, and even the wranglers. That was part of the problem. There were too many people who could have easily arranged the accidents.

The film would go on, though. There was too much time, too much money, too much effort already invested to stop now. The credits would now include a line dedicating *West Wind*:

"To the memory of Mick O'Connell."

TWELVE

Despite Mick's death, only a few scenes in *West Wind* had to be changed. Most of his important scenes had already been shot and could be used. His character, Lenny, was supposed to die in a car wreck near the end of the movie. The setup scenes for that were already finished. They could shoot around him for the remainder of the picture. As a grim John told the Phillipses, "It seems rough, but that's how it works. Mick isn't the first actor to die during filming."

Several days after the memorial service they held for Mick on the ranch, they had to shoot the scene set immediately after Lenny's death. It was labeled "Lenny's Farewell" on the production board. It would have been a difficult scene in any case. The night before, Tim had told Sam he wasn't sure he could do it. Now she watched quietly from the side as they did take after take, seldom getting halfway through the scene.

All through the picture, Jeb and Lenny were supposed to have been both buddies and rivals. They had grown closer in the shared danger of the cliffside rescue. They had competed in rodeos. Now Lenny's life was cut off by the wreck, and Jeb was reacting, facing the reality of death for the first time. It was a pivotal scene, the emotional climax of the movie as Jeb grows up.

Nicole's make-up needed frequent repair, as genuine tears kept damaging it. Her part in the scene was minor; the focus was on Tim. He couldn't do it. There were too many parallels between the script and real life. An hour crept by as the same dialogue, with all its overtones of reality, was spoken again and again by Tim. John, his voice quiet, called for another take.

"One more take. One more, dammit!" Tim stood in the center of the corral, glaring at John. "And that is *it*, Ryder. I can't take any more of this crap."

"Then give me some emotion this time,"

John answered, his voice still quiet. "I've seen more feeling from a crash dummy."

Tim's voice broke. "John, I can't do it. I can't!"

"Yes, you can!" The director's voice cracked like a whip. John waited for a moment. "We all feel it. Now make the camera feel it so the audience will feel it! Mick was a professional. He would have done it. Now are you an actor, or are you just a star?" Sarcasm dripped from the last word.

Tim stood rigid. Then he nodded once, a tight, controlled motion. At John's nod, the call went out for silence. His voice was barely audible as he called, "All right, let's roll, please." The echo of "Rolling!" came. "Marker . . . set . . . action!"

"Jeb, he . . . he's gone." Nicole's voice was choked.

"No. He can't be." Tim's line started low, and rose in pitch to a final shout. *"No-o-o!"*

The scene continued. This time, Tim put his own grief and rage into the part. Tears were streaming down Sam's face. Tim reached the point where John had stopped him several times and kept going. Sam saw John motioning to the cinematographer to keep rolling. Tim's voice cracked as he got to the end of the scene, and he broke down.

"Cut!" John stood up. "Tim, that was what I wanted. I knew you could do it."

"You're satisfied? You wanted this? You . . ." Tim broke off and headed for the edge of the corral, then he whirled and began swearing. He cussed John and the production and himself, then sprinted away.

Sam started to go after him, but John stopped her. "Sam. Let him go." She halted, and he caught up with her. Putting an arm around her shoulders, he said, "Let him work it out on his own. I know Tim. Right now he needs to be alone."

"But . . . I . . ." She turned to John, biting her lip.

"He'll be all right," he said. His face was wet with sweat and tears. "I think he needed to do that scene. It's the best he's ever done." He stared in the direction Tim had taken toward his own trailer. "Mick would have been proud of him."

Sam stayed and talked with John a while longer. He and Sylvie had intended to announce their engagement officially at the wrap party, normally held after a movie was completed. Now John told Sam he wondered if it would be better to cancel the party. He felt personally responsible for Mick's death, although there wasn't anything he could have done to prevent it.

Sam didn't think canceling the party or the announcement was a good idea. There had been so much bad news recently; Sam thought the party would lift everyone's spirits. They were arguing about it when Nicole came out of her dressing room. She had removed the last traces of her tear-smudged make-up and was dry-eyed again. John greeted her, then excused himself and headed for the house.

"Where's Tim?" Nicole asked.

"Still in his trailer, I guess," Sam said. "I'm going over there in a little while. John said I should give him some time."

"Yeah," Nicole agreed readily. "We've all been through a lot the past month, but that scene today . . ." She shuddered. "I don't ever want to have to hurt like that during a scene again. I don't care if it won me an Oscar—I couldn't hack it."

"I almost couldn't watch," Sam admitted.

"And at the same time, I couldn't *not* watch. I've never seen Tim act that way."

"That's because he never has before. He's a better actor for it. Now, any time he needs to, he'll be able to pull that emotion out of himself." Nicole was silent for a moment, then added, "But I'll bet Tim would give up acting entirely if it'd bring Mick back."

They started to walk, following the path John had taken. Hesitantly, Sam asked the question that was keeping her awake at night. "Nicole, do you think Helen did it?" The double had stayed at her lodging in town for the last few days. Rick had hired another double to cover the remaining scenes, but Sheriff McBride had asked her not to leave town.

"Absolutely not," Nicole said, shaking her head violently. "Sammie, I know you didn't like what she said about Tim, but that girl's too timid even to try that sort of thing. The only time she doesn't jump at her own shadow is when she's on a horse. I like Tim, but he hurt that kid."

"That's the problem," Sam said. "The note Tim got said he wasn't going to hurt anyone else. Helen was hurt."

"I still don't believe it. She might have written the letter. But there's no way you're going to convince me she planned those accidents."

"Then who did?" Sam demanded. "They weren't accidents—they can prove that now. Those ropes were sabotaged. Do you think Tim rigged them as a publicity stunt? John? Rick?"

"No, of course not." Nicole stopped.

"You see the problem." Sam was talking to herself more than Nicole. "I don't think they did either, even if the sheriff does. If it wasn't just publicity, that means the letter probably is tied in. Which means whoever did it feels hurt by Tim."

Nicole looked sideways at Sam. "At least now you admit Helen got hurt."

"I'm not blaming Tim." Sam was quick to defend him. "Maybe she imagined more romance than there was."

"Yeah. Maybe she imagined things," Nicole drawled. "Maybe other people do, too. How badly do you think you'll get hurt?"

Sam stopped and faced her. "Not at all." She knew she wasn't telling the truth, but it wasn't a total lie, either. At the moment, there was such an air of fantasy over everything that it would be easy to pretend she'd imagined the whole summer.

Nicole shook her head. "Yeah, sure." She changed the subject. "Speaking of hurt, how's Jackie?"

Sam grimaced. "She's a mess." They walked on in silence.

When they reached Tim's trailer, Nicole said, "Sammie, I told you before, no one knows where that Kiss of Death tag came from. Tim's got a reputation for being major bad luck regardless of where it started. He says he's never hurt anyone, but we know Helen got hurt when she fell for him. And Mick and Walt are dead. And you think about the way Jackie's feeling. Just remember, I warned you."

"Come in," Tim called when Sam knocked at the door of his trailer. Sam entered, unsure of her reception. His voice sounded tired, and he was sprawled on the small couch listlessly. As she stood in the door, he moved over, making room for her beside him. She sat down. That answered that question; he wasn't going to run her off—yet.

She was afraid he wouldn't like what she was going to say. "Tim?" Before she could frame the question, she was in his arms. He kissed her, almost desperately, then held her. He hugged her tightly, so tightly she could feel his heart beating. She stroked the back of his head, smoothing the silky blond hair, comforting him like a child. Tim wasn't interested in romance right now, just in the warmth of her embrace.

At last he released her. Sam watched him from the corner of her eyes as he sighed and leaned back. This wasn't going to be easy, but she had to ask him about all the rumors.

Before she could say anything, he spoke. "I almost lost it completely out there today," he said, looking straight ahead. "All I could think about was that I was alive and Mick was dead, and it wasn't supposed to be that way. Do you know the only thing that kept me out there? Whoever it was that killed Mick—it was murder, I don't care who it was aimed at—wants me dead. Well, I'm not. And I'm going to find out who it was, if it's the last thing I do."

"Don't you have any idea who it was?" Sam asked.

"Stop asking me that!" He shouted, startling her. Lowering his voice somewhat, he went on. "Everyone keeps asking me that. The sheriff, John, Nicole, Dave, you. My agent even phoned and asked! Somebody raked up the tabloid that had that Kiss of Death nonsense in it."

She jumped, but he didn't notice.

"All that crap about me being a jinx, and girls dying because of me . . . It was worse than most tabloid articles. My uncle wanted to sue, but I wouldn't let him." Tim's eyes were haunted. "I never did understand why they printed those lies, but you can imagine what it was like trying to explain it to Sheriff McBride."

Sam could. The sheriff wasn't an imaginative man and he would be ready to think the worst of Tim—or any actor, for that matter. Even Mick wasn't exempt—Jackie wouldn't have been hurt if she hadn't fallen in love with an actor. From what the sheriff had said, Sam knew he thought it had been planned for publicity and had gone too far. Vague tabloid reports fit right in with that theory.

"And now there's this." He pulled her to her feet and went over to the dresser. "Take a look, but don't touch it. I suppose I'm going to have to give it to McBride."

A note lay on the dresser, printed in pencil on a sheet of paper. The paper had the production company's logo on it; anyone could have gotten a piece from the office. The precise block capitals said: "You bring death to too many. It won't miss you forever."

Sam looked at him in horror. "When—"

"Right before I had to go do that scene," he said tiredly. "Do you see why I was so upset? It wasn't just Mick. It's because whoever it was intends to keep trying." He sat back down and leaned back, eyes closed. "I don't want anyone else hurt. Especially not you, Sam. You'd better leave. I'm starting to really feel like a kiss of death."

She dropped down beside him on the couch. "You aren't," she said, taking his hand. "And I'm not leaving."

Filming was almost over now. With the completion of "Lenny's Farewell," all that was left were a few short scenes that had been squeezed out of the schedule due to the delays. As Sam set out the rolls for lunch on Thursday, she wondered if the next day really would be the last time. By the weekend most of the cast would be gone. Once they left, the number they were feeding would drop drastically, and her mother had said Sam's help would no longer be needed. Tim had said nothing about leaving yet, and she didn't think the sheriff would let Helen leave. He wanted Tim to remain as well, although legally he had no hold.

"Sam." She looked over her shoulder at the familiar voice. Paul stood there, a platter of cold cuts in his hands. He handed it to her. "Your mom said you were over here. You forgot this, so she asked me to bring it over."

"Yeah, I guess I did." Sam set the platter down by the rolls. She wondered if he'd say why he'd really come by. One thing she was sure of, Paul hadn't come out to carry cold cuts for her. "How's it going?" she asked.

"All right." There was a long pause as she got the other serving trays off the cart. "I just wanted to talk to you."

"I have to be here for lunch—" she began, when Aunt Sylvie came up.

"I'll manage by myself, Sammie." Aunt Sylvie took the serving ladle from Sam's suddenly numb fingers and gently pushed her toward Paul. "I think you owe Paul a talk, at least."

Sam followed Paul out of the tent, gritting her teeth to keep her words under control. What she wanted to say to Aunt Sylvie she'd say later, in private. Sam was furious with her. She hadn't interfered in her aunt's life at all. Why did everyone in the world think it was okay to tell Sam how to run her life?

Once they were out of earshot of anyone else,

Paul turned to her and said, "Look, I didn't mean to force this on you. I just told your aunt and mom I wanted to talk to you, and they sent me down with that tray, and . . . well . . ."

Sam clenched her teeth for a moment, then sighed. "Yeah, I saw. It wasn't your fault." She stopped. It might not have been his fault, but that didn't mean she wanted to talk with him.

With surprising gentleness, he reached out and turned her toward him. He looked directly into her eyes as he said, "I miss you, Sam. I never said so, I guess maybe because I didn't know how to, but you're part of my life. If you don't want me in your life anymore, I'll leave you alone." His grip tightened slightly, and he said, "You've got to tell me, Sam. I won't let you just walk away from me like there was never anything between us."

Her throat tightened as she realized what he'd just said: *Just walk away like there was never anything . . .* That was what so many had accused Tim of doing. Tim had almost admitted it the night before, when he'd talked about Helen. It was easier to walk away without a word, but it wasn't fair to the one left behind, left dangling and hoping. Tim might leave her behind that way. It would almost be fair, if he treated her the way she was treating Paul.

"I won't say I'm not jealous—I am." His eyes were almost pleading now. "If you tell me you're happy with Tim, I won't say another word. But," he repeated, more intently, "you have to *say* something! I won't just let it drift. Tell me to stay, or tell me to go to hell, whatever. Just say something."

"I will," she whispered. It was a promise, and she'd keep it. "Paul, please, let me have a day or two to think. He'll be leaving soon, and with . . . with Mick's accident and everything else that's happened . . . I don't know!" she finished desperately. "Give me just a few days more. Please." Her voice sank back to a whisper.

He looked at her for another moment, then said, "All right, Sam. A few more days." Abruptly, he pulled her to him. It was the first time he'd held her since Walt's funeral. His large hands caressed her back, warm through her blouse. Briefly, he bent to kiss her, with all the old sweetness. Then he held her close again. In a low voice, he said, "But I swear, if that damned actor hurts you, I'll kill him!"

"Don't say that, Paul," Sam spat, breaking free of his arms. "Don't ever say that."

"Make up your mind, Sam." Without another word, he turned and marched away.

THIRTEEN

Later that evening, Sam went out to Tim's trailer. She had to face him, the way Paul had faced her. She'd spent the day thinking hard. Sam knew now that movie stars weren't just characters out of fairy tales but people who worked hard at a grinding, tedious job. As much fun as it was to watch for a short time, it wasn't her job or her world. Her life was right here on the ranch.

She remembered the time she and Paul had spent most of one moonless night up on Lee's Flat, watching the stars and listening to the night noises. They had heard the distant whisper of jets passing far overhead, on their way to Tucson or places even farther away.

Mostly there had been insect sounds and night-calling birds, and the serenade of a coyote pack. There was no glare of city lights, no blast of sound. Just silence and stars.

This was the world she loved, the only one she wanted. And she knew Tim would never be a part of it. He enjoyed it as an occasional treat, the way she enjoyed a shopping trip to the city. But his heart would always be in his work. He'd grown up on movie sets the way she had on the Lizardfoot, and they were his real home.

Knowing this didn't make it any easier to face Tim. When his arms were around her, it was hard to think of anything besides the way she felt right then. Maybe that was more important than thinking about worlds and homes and the reality of school and family.

And maybe not.

Tim was just leaving his trailer when she got there. "Hi, Sam." He kissed her, and her knees wobbled with her resolve. How could she give this up? He didn't know what was going through her mind and released her after an all-too-short moment.

"I was just going to go over to see Worthless one last time," he said, showing her the apple he had. "They're supposed to ship him home tomorrow. You know, I think I've ridden him more and seen more of him in the last month than I have since I bought him."

She fell into step beside him. There it was again—the differences between their lives. She couldn't imagine owning a horse she couldn't ride whenever she felt like it. Tim loved Worthless, but sometimes he'd go months without seeing him. That was no way to own a horse.

"I'll split it and you can give Twigs the other half," he said. He took her hand as they walked, just as he had on so many other evenings. Sam was as nervous as though she were about to enter the arena for the National Rodeo Championship.

Waiting wouldn't make it easier. Just before they got to the barn, she stopped him and said, "Tim, what happens next?"

"Well, they ship Worthless home tomorrow. All the scenes with the cast are nearly done. It'll take them less than a week to finish up the odds and ends. Then they start editing—"

"That's not what I meant, Tim." She spoke quietly, but this time she wasn't going to be distracted. She'd drifted for too long. "What happens about us?"

He was silent for a moment. Then he put his arms around her and said, "I love you, Sam." He started to kiss her, but she pulled free of his embrace.

"I know you do," she said. Her voice was shaky as she continued. "That isn't an answer, though."

His hands fell limply to his side. "I've always tried not to make any promises," he said, staring into her eyes. "Too many times I can't keep them. I can't promise I'll always love you. I'm not ready yet."

Her eyes stung with sudden tears. It was an honest answer, painfully honest. "I don't think I am either, Tim. And we won't even be together after tomorrow. You're leaving then, aren't you?" She pushed open the barn door and they went in.

"Yeah. I'm sorry, Sam." It was the first time he'd admitted what they both knew, that he'd be leaving soon. He pulled out a pocketknife and cut the apple in half. "I'd like to see you again." He went back to Worthless's stall. He fed the half apple to the black gelding, soothing him and patting his neck, while Sam fed the other half to Twigs. Both of the horses were restless and whickered uneasily. Sam wondered what had the animals spooked.

"I do have to get back home," Tim said. "My agent has a couple of scripts he wants me to look at, and I want to ask John about the editing —I've never bothered with that before, but I have money in this one myself—and I need to spend some time with Uncle Bill, but in a few weeks I think I could get back out to visit."

"Sure." A new voice came from behind them. "Like you always come back to visit."

Tim and Sam turned, Tim saying, "Hi, Dave." Then his voice died and he pulled Sam to his side, an arm around her. Dave Jeffries stood in the door of an empty stall on the other side of the barn. In his hands, pointed at them, was a shotgun.

"I'm through messing around with accidents," he said. He held the gun rock-steady. "You just keep hurting everyone all around you and you never get hurt yourself."

"Did you get that from props?" Tim asked. He obviously didn't think so; he was pushing Sam behind him as he spoke.

"It's real, Tim. You're the phony." Dave's voice was ragged and his breathing labored, as though he'd been running. Sam recognized her father's gun. Normally it was kept behind the kitchen door, shells on the shelf above it, ready to use on rattlesnakes. Dave must have stolen it from the house.

Tim pushed in front of Sam so she was wedged between him and the door of Worthless's stall. The gelding put his head over the door and whuffled down the side of her neck. "Dave, I'm an actor," Tim said. He was acting now, showing a confidence he didn't have. Sam could feel him trembling as hard as she was herself. "That doesn't make me a phony any more than it makes you one. You're in the same business yourself."

"You don't do all your acting in front of a camera," Dave said. He advanced a couple of steps toward them, the double-barreled shotgun never wavering. "I'm talking about the acting you do off-camera, like telling Sam you'd come back. The acting you do when you hurt people. When you kill them."

"I haven't killed anyone, Dave. You have. You killed Mick." Tim tried to keep between the gun and Sam, in a futile gesture of protection.

"That should have been you!" Dave yelled. His face twisted as he fought tears. "You always walk away; someone else always dies. This time, you're going to be the one, Tim."

"Why?" Tim almost whispered the question. "Why have you been doing this, Dave? I thought we were friends."

"I warned you," Dave said. "That letter. I said I'd make sure you never hurt anyone else again, and now Walt's dead, and Mick's dead. And it's *your fault*, Tim! Just like it was your fault when Ramona died."

"Oh, my God." Tim swayed slightly. "Oh my God, *Ramona*—"

"Yeah, Ramona." Dave spoke in a monotone now. "Did you ever tell Sam about Ramona? About the way you killed her? About the way you left her like you're fixing to leave—"

"I didn't kill her!" Tim shouted. "She killed herself! I didn't even know about it till months later." He swallowed, fighting tears. "It was over between us a long time before she killed herself."

"A month," Dave interrupted. "One lousy month. You didn't care how you hurt people then and you still don't. When I met Helen before the production started and found out how you treated her, I knew you'd never change and

I decided to pay you back. You killed Ramona just as sure as if you'd shot her."

Sam tried to push past Tim, as Worthless slobbered down her neck again. Her throat was so dry she couldn't swallow, but she had to make Dave think. Maybe the reminder that Tim wasn't alone would make him hesitate. Tim blocked her, as he said, "When I heard about it later, I cried. I don't care if you believe me or not. It wasn't my fault. She called for help to some guy who didn't come."

"Me," Dave said. His voice rose to a shriek. "Me! I was her boyfriend before you ever showed up. I was still mad—I didn't think she really meant it when she called and said she'd poisoned herself. I didn't go." His voice fell and he raised the shotgun. "She sent me a letter before she took those pills. She couldn't get over you, and you didn't come back. Your fault, Tim, all your fault."

The click as he cocked both barrels sounded like a thunderclap. Sam froze and felt Tim stiffen in front of her as Dave aimed the shotgun. He held it leveled at Tim, nestled against his shoulder in a way that told of long experience with such weapons. "Tim, move away from Sam," Dave ordered. "Walk toward the front, up by those bales of hay. I don't want to hurt the horses. Sam, you follow him. Don't get in the way—I don't want to hurt you, but I will if I have to."

Slowly, Tim took a step away from the stall, and then another. Both horses were moving uneasily, whinnying as they smelled the fear and hatred in the air. Twigs, normally as placid as an old plow horse, kicked the walls. The thud of hooves hitting wood sounded unnaturally loud. Dave gestured sharply with the shotgun, and Sam followed Tim. Dave came behind, the barrel steady and only inches behind her.

For a moment, she thought wildly about turning and throwing herself on the gun, letting Tim run for it. But he wouldn't. Besides, any sudden moves and Dave would snap completely.

They reached the bales at the front of the barn and stopped. Sam and Tim turned to face the gun. All they could do was try to postpone death for as long as possible. They had brushed past it so many times this summer. Maybe they could do it once more.

"You'll never get away with it," Tim said. His voice was steady now, as though he'd moved past fear.

"I don't care. After I kill you, I'll kill myself

anyway. Nothing matters to me anymore. You're going to pay, Tim." Dave raised the shotgun again. "Get out of the way, Sam."

She shook her head, stepping over to stand beside Tim. "No. You'll have to kill us both."

"No!" Tim yelled. His voice cracked and he tried to push her aside, as Dave said, "Sam, I don't want to hurt you."

"Then don't." Paul stood in the open door, behind Dave. For the first time, the deadly twin barrels dropped away from them, as Dave half-turned his head in shock. "Put down the shotgun, Dave. Now."

"No!" Dave jerked the gun back into line and pulled the double trigger, just as Paul reached him and grabbed him from behind. Almost at the same instant, Tim pushed Sam behind the baled hay and dived over it himself. The shot went wild, slamming into the boards behind them. Sam's cheek stung as a splinter torn loose by the shot ripped into it. Dave and Paul were fighting for the gun. Sam scrambled to her feet as Tim climbed onto the bale and dived head-long at the struggling pair. His tackle knocked them both off their feet, and the three sprawled on the ground as Sam hurried toward them.

Suddenly, Paul grunted as Dave drove the

butt of the shotgun deep into his stomach. Dave kicked wildly at Tim, knocking him back, and raced for the open door. Tim shook his head like a groggy fighter, then got to his feet, his mouth bleeding. He ran after Dave.

Sam bent over Paul, who was doubled over, curled around his pain. "I'm okay!" Paul gasped. "Help Tim!" For an instant, she hesitated. She heard the roar of a truck engine coming to life. Then she whirled and ran to the door, coming to an abrupt stop as she saw what was happening outside.

Dave was in her pickup; once again, she'd forgotten to take the keys out. He accelerated, gravel spurting from beneath the tires, just as Tim threw himself over the tailgate. She held her breath as Tim crawled forward and swung out on the right side of the cab, ready to crawl through the window. It was right out of one of his films. But this time Tim was doing it himself, and there were no cameras rolling. The truck picked up speed, heading for the gate and the road to town, while people came shouting from the ranch house and the living trailers.

Then the truck started to lose speed while the engine raced even faster. Sam sobbed once and ran toward the truck, now coasting to a halt in neutral while the engine screamed and Tim clung to the side, halfway around. Dave had never driven the Green Beast and didn't know its peculiarities. It was hung up between gears.

The engine died with a shudder. Around the yard, people converged on the truck. They slowed as the truck stopped. Tim dropped off the side of the stalled vehicle, and Sam ran to him. Behind her, Paul came out of the barn, still holding his stomach, and joined them.

Inside the cab, Dave sat motionless, staring forward, clenching the steering wheel. A dozen people or more surrounded the truck, watching him. No one spoke. Then, slowly, as the silence held, he started to weep and his head dropped onto his hands. It was over.

A week later, Sam and Paul drove Tim to the airport in Tucson. Dave was in jail, and the trial looked like a mere formality. He had confessed to everything. The remaining questions had all been answered by that time.

When Sam had asked Paul how he'd managed to show up at the barn at just the right moment, he'd smiled and even blushed a little.

"Well, Sammie," Paul had said. "I'm not so sure I want to tell you that."

"Don't tell me—you just sensed it," Sam guessed.

"Close, but not exactly." Paul put his arm around her shoulder. "Actually I was spying on you and Tim. When you didn't come out of the barn, I went in there to break things up."

"You shouldn't have been snooping on me, Paul," Sam said, knocking his arm away. "But I'm glad you were."

Tim had answered the next question. Ramona had been his first serious girlfriend, and he admitted that he had walked away from her. He'd never known how hard she'd taken it. Her last letter to Dave had been found in his trailer on the ranch. The tragic part of it all, Sam thought, was that if Dave had ever admitted his own guilt, Walt and Mick wouldn't have died. Ramona had called for help and Dave had ignored her until it was too late. To ease his pain, he focused all the blame on Tim. Ramona's suicide had been the first link in a chain of tragedy.

It was all such a waste. Jackie was still in mourning for Mick, and Sam knew she would never be the same. There were empty places in so many lives, in Agua Verde and beyond. All because of a summer romance gone wrong two years before.

It was time to put the past to rest now. If Dave had been able to do so, none of this would have happened.

They stood in the terminal, waiting for the call to board. The flight was already half an hour late. Tim glanced at Paul, then asked Sam, "Will I see you at the wedding?"

"Only if you come back to Arizona," she said. "Aunt Sylvie's convinced John it'll be easier to have it at the ranch. They're planning to spend a few weeks there after they get back from Honolulu and the honeymoon; then she's moving to Hollywood with him. I may go visit her sometime."

"I hope you do," he said, with another glance at Paul. "Will you call me when you get there?"

Sam nodded. "I will." As she said it, she slipped her hand into Paul's. She'd always remember Tim, and she hoped they'd always be friends. The romance was over.

He glanced down at their clasped hands. With a half-smile he said, "Just as a friend."

Paul added, "Friends." They all smiled.

The loudspeaker rose over the hum of voices in the waiting area. "Delta flight one-fifty-one, now boarding at gate twelve for Los Angeles." That was Tim's flight. There was a general stir, as those boarding moved toward the gate. Tim took Sam's free hand and said, "You know, this has never happened before."

"What hasn't?" She thought she knew what he meant, but waited for him to explain.

"I never realized it before," Tim said, confirming her guess. "I was always the one to end things. Only I never had the guts to just tell someone it was over. Maybe if I had, Ramona wouldn't have died, and Walt, and Mick—"

"And maybe something else would have happened," she interrupted. "Don't start with maybes, Tim. Aunt Sylvie always says, *'Might be never was.'*"

He sighed. "She's right. But I'm glad you didn't leave me wondering. Good-bye, Sam." For the last time, he took her into his arms and kissed her.

He shook Paul's hand, then turned and walked down the jetway. Sam and Paul moved to the big windows at the end of the lounge and stood, arms around each other, watching until the plane took off and vanished into the western sky.

Then, hand in hand, they left the terminal. It was a long drive back to Agua Verde and the Lizardfoot Ranch.